"I be Tamar," the strange woman said cheerfully. "Though there be others hereabouts as have other names for me. And thou art?"

"I'm Judy Wade," Judy replied promptly. "This is my brother Crockett. And that's my sister, Holly. We've just come to live at Dimsdale."

"Dimsdale," repeated Tamar. Now her smile was gone. "Aye, I be forgetting once again. That be not the Dimsdale that was, but the Dimsdale which *is* which thee knows. Still lies the shadow." She shook her head regretfully. "Still lies the cruel shadow. . . ."

Holly's uneasiness prompted her to speak up, "Where is this—this house? Grandma and Grandpa, they never told us about it, or you!"

"This house be where it has always been," Tamar answered quietly. "It was, is, and will be—for it be of the earth and gifts of the earth."

LAVENDER-GREEN MAGIC

ANDRE NORTON

Illustrated by Judith Gwyn Brown

ace books

A Division of Charter Communications Inc.
A GROSSET & DUNLAP COMPANY
1120 Avenue of the Americas
New York, New York 10036

An ACE Book by arrangement with Thomas Y. Crowell Company

Designed by Karen Bernath

First ACE printing: March 1977
Printed in U.S.A.

ANDRE NORTON, one of Ace Books' most respected and prolific authors—with over fifty books and millions of copies in print—is world renowned for her uncanny ability to create tightly plotted action stories based on her extensive readings in travel, archeology, anthropology, natural history, folklore and psycho-esper research. With classic understatement belied by the enthusiastic critical reception of all her books, she has described herself as ". . . rather a very staid teller of old fashioned stories . . ."

Miss Norton began her literary career as an editor for her high school paper and quickly progressed to writing, publishing her first book before the age of twenty-one. After graduating from Western University, and working for the Library of Congress for a number of years, she began her writing career in earnest, consistently producing science fiction novels of the highest quality.

Miss Norton presently resides in Florida under the careful management of her feline associates.

JUDITH GWYN BROWN is the illustrator of many distinguished books, including *Mandy*, *Daisy*, and *The Best Christmas Pageant Ever*. She has also written a book of her own and illustrated it. She particularly enjoyed the combination of reality and fantasy that *Lavender-Green Magic* required. Ms. Brown studied art history at New York University before deciding to become an illustrator, and her fine pen technique reveals her familiarity with earlier masters of graphic art. She lives and works in New York City, where she was born and grew up.

For Mrs. Lena May Lanier,

who through her stories

introduced me to the Wades

Contents

LAVENDER-
GREEN MAGIC

1 Dimsdale

Rain beat against the windows of the bus so hard one could barely see out. The wind was so strong that sometimes the whole of the big coach shivered when a blast caught it head on.

Inside, those same windows were all steamed. And it smelled. It smelled of the banana the little boy in the seat ahead of Holly had been eating, of wet clothes belonging to the people who had gotten on at the last two stops. It smelled just of people.

Holly wanted to be sick but she was not going to let herself. Only babies got travel-sick. She held her mouth tight shut, swallowing and swallowing. As she pressed her hands forcibly against her middle, she scowled fiercely at the world.

It was easy to scowl, everything was so hateful. Not only the storm outside but the bus, why they were on it, everything in the world—that world which had come to pieces all around them so that there was nothing safe or happy or as it should be any more. She swallowed again. No, she was *not* going to be sick, and she was not going to cry as Judy had been doing off and on for what seemed like days now, weeks, months—

Crock, Crockett Wade, had been trying to see through the steamed window, wiping impatiently to clear a pane which almost immediately fogged over again. Now he thumped back in his seat, turned his head to regard his sister Holly.

"What's the matter with you?" he demanded.

She dug her elbow into his ribs, banging her arm on the seat divider between them in the process.

"Nothing!" She gestured warningly at the two seats behind, where Mom and Judy sat. "Nothing at all."

He stared at her and then appeared to get the message. "Sure," he said in a lower voice, "Sussex stop can't be much farther now."

Holly did not know whether he was trying to raise his own spirits by that hope, or hers. At that moment she did not care. All that mattered was that she was *not* going to be sick! Not Holly Wade, who was no baby.

Then she heard Mom's voice from behind, though she would not turn to look, for fear Mom would guess how she felt. Mom had enough on her mind without having to worry about a girl who was already in the sixth grade and surely old enough to look after her ownself.

"Next stop, Holly, Crock. I wish this rain would let up a little."

Suddenly Holly did not want it to be the next stop, in spite of how she felt; she wanted to ride on and on because when they got off, why, they would be there. Not at home any more—but among strangers in a place where they would have to stay whether they liked it or not.

Ever since that telegram had come—

Holly squinted her eyelids together, hard. Just as she was not going to be sick, she was not going to cry, either. Only she could not push away the memory of the telegram. Mom—Mom had sat down so quick with it in her hands, as if she were afraid to open it. And when she had—no, Holly would *not* remember how Mom had looked when she read it.

"Staff Sergeant Joel Wade missing in action"—that's how it had read. Mom seemed to shrink down in her chair just as if she had the "miseries" inside her, as old Auntie Ada was always saying. Then she straightened up again, and there were calls to the Red Cross, and to other people who just might know something. Only nobody did.

Finally Mom told them they would have to make plans. She was going to be a nurse again and she had a place in the Pine Mount Rest Home. That was not in Boston, where they had been living ever since Daddy had gone to Vietnam, but in the country farther upstate.

3 ❧

Judy was the one who had asked the question which had been in all their minds after Mom had told them that: "Do—do we go to live there too, Mom?"

Mom had been smiling, as if she wanted them all to know that her getting the job was a good thing, one to be glad about. Nor did she stop smiling when she shook her head and told them of the rest of the hateful, hateful plan.

"No. It is a place for older people, Bunny." (Bunny was a joke name Daddy had given Judy because she was born on Easter, and he said the Bunny must have forgotten his basket of eggs and brought her instead.)

"Then—then where *are* we going?" Crockett wanted to know. Holly just stood there, an awful coldness inside her making her feel as if she was out in the winter winds without any clothes on.

"You are going to live with Grandpa and Grandma Wade in Sussex. It is close enough to Pine Mount so I can come and see you when I have my time off."

"No!" Holly had exploded then and she did not care. "No—"

Mom was no longer smiling when she looked at Holly, she was very quiet-faced as she always looked when one of them was a big disappointment. But Holly, with that strange cold all through her now, did not even care about that. She—Mom must be there, with them! If she went away—she might be "missing" too!

"Yes, Holly," Mom had continued. "It's the best plan for us. I shall have a good job, they find it difficult to get nurses at the Mount. The place is too quiet for most of the younger girls who want time off where there is something amusing to do. So the pay is better than I would get here in town. I know that you will have a very good home with Grandpa and Grandma. They are so pleased to think you are coming."

Holly wanted to shout out "No" again, but she did not quite dare. So she swallowed that "No," just as she was swallowing and swallowing right now. Everything had moved so quickly, renting the house to the Elands (the Wades did not even take their furniture, only their clothes, and some things like Crock's stamp collection, Judy's box of cloth pieces, and her own best-loved books). Now they were on their way—almost there—to a hateful place, with the rain crying and the wind howling. Just as Holly wanted so desperately to howl and cry her ownself.

She could not even remember now what Grandpa and Grandma looked like. Until Daddy had gone to Vietnam, the Wades had lived in places near the army camps, and those had been too far away from Sussex for any visiting. Grandpa and Grandma were not used to traveling, Daddy had told them. He had wanted to take the family back to Sussex himself this past summer. Then he had been sent overseas and they never went. All Holly could remember now of her grandparents was a picture Daddy had shown them—a picture of two strangers.

They never had letters from Grandpa. But Grandma had always written once a week. Big writing on one sheet of paper which had lines on it like a school tablet. She never said much, mostly about how she was piecing a quilt, or canning food to eat, or things like that.

At Christmas time they had always sent a box with things in it which were strange, too. Such as that set of doll dishes for Judy all made of wood, and a tiny, tiny basket that Mom said had been carved out of a nut. For Crock there were some soldiers and a dog made of wood. And she had had a tote bag last year made all of bright pieces of patchwork. She had thought it was rather silly and tried to hide it. But Mom made her carry it to school. Then all the girls in her class wanted to know where she got it, and it turned out to be quite an exciting present, after all. Mom had gotten a lot of little bottles, all filled with dried leaves and flower petals. She used some of them when she cooked, and some to make closets smell nice.

But all had been different kinds of presents than those Holly had seen in the stores in Boston. She was sure that Sussex was a very different kind of place to live. A place where she was not going to want to live!

Now the bus was slowing down. Holly wished with all her might this stop was not theirs. But wishing got you nowhere, not when the world had come apart around you. She had pulled on her raincoat when Mom had warned them; now she buttoned it and drew her plastic rain hat over her hair, tying it as firmly as she could under her chin.

The blast which hit them as they climbed down was so fierce it left them gasping. They ran as fast as they could for the door of the store before which the bus had come to a stop, and hurried in. Luckily they did not have to drag any luggage with them (Mom had sent that all on ahead), but Holly felt as if someone had poured a teacup of water down her back, another down her front, and that both were now dripping into her boots.

"Come in, folks." A lady had opened the door of the store when she saw them coming and now stood there shaking her head, while white hair fluffed up so wildly around her face it seemed just like a growth of dandelion seeds all ready to blow away.

She was a lot shorter than Mom, and she wore a sweater about her shoulders. But that was not buttoned over the big white apron which covered most of her front. She had slammed the door shut as soon as they were all through it, and now shook her head so that her fine white hair looked more flyaway than ever as she peered into the street where the bus was growling off on its way again.

"This is a day like to drown ducks," she announced as she turned back to stare at them as if they *were* the ducks. "My, now, you have got yourselves wet, an' just on that littly bitty run, too. . . . No, ma'am"—she spoke to Mom, who was staying as near as she could to the door and motioning Judy and Crock back to stand nearer to her—"don't you never mind 'bout a little drippin'. On a day like this enough comes in that door every time it opens to make a real wave or two. The few sprinkles you brought don't make a mite of difference."

The lady reached behind a pillar on which hung some long-handled brushes tied in a bunch, two strings of dried onions, and a calendar, and she pulled out a mop. This she applied vigorously to the floor, where the storm had indeed driven some runnels of water under the door itself.

"Now then"—she talked as she worked—"what can I do for you folks? Someone coming to meet you here? Or you thinking of getting Jim Backus to taxi you? Don't think that'll work. Jim, he gets a lotta calls—see there?"

The lady loosed the mop with one hand and waved toward a wall phone. Beside that was thumbtacked a strip of paper almost covered with scrawled words and numbers. "Them, all of them, mind you, have been asking for Jim an' he ain't called in for nigh on to an hour now. So he won't be back in any hurry."

Holly had been looking around the store. This cluttered room was quite unlike the supermarket where she did errands for Mom at home. Yet there were even more things stacked, hung, piled around so you could not tell whether it was a grocery store—as the shelves lined with canned goods and packages, the small glass-fronted meat and cheese case, the bin of potatoes, suggested—or something quite different. Because, on the other side, there was a rack of dresses hanging limply from their hangers as if they felt sorry to find themselves there; a table on which thick flannelly looking shirts were piled; a row of boots (not smartly smooth fitting ones like her own, which had been her birthday gift last month, but big rubber ones into which she, or at least Judy, could fit both feet and legs at once). The shelves on that side had bolts of cloth on them. There was a small case holding braid, and zippers, like in a sewing shop.

There were smells aplenty, too. Ones Holly could recognize, such as coffee, and cheese. While at the back was a kind of cage with a sign over a square window: U.S. Post Office!

The big room was warm after the chill of the rain, but not stuffy, smelly warm as it had been on the bus. Now the lady gave a last slip-slap of her mop, pushed it back into hiding, and repeated, "You wanting Jim, ma'am?"

"I believe my father-in-law will meet us. Mr. Wade, Mr. Luther Wade—" Mom was smiling her polite company smile, but Holly sensed something was not quite right. Mom looked her usual self. She had on the red rain-and-shine coat Daddy had bought her (he said to be cheerful for gray days) and red boots like Holly's. Now she had taken off her rain bonnet, so her crisp black hair looked pretty again. Mom was pretty, her smooth brown skin and her hair all combed up like that. The beauty-shop lady had called Mom's hair set a "modified Afro." Holly sighed. It would probably be years before she could wear hers that way.

No, Mom looked just right. And Crock, he had on his good slacks and his trench coat. And Judy—Judy, who had a dimple in her cheek and her hair all carefully braided—wore her brown coat and her own boots. Holly had on her yellow raincoat and her hair was neat, too. They all made what Dad would say was a "right smart appearance."

"Well now," the store lady was saying, "so you're old Lute's kinfolk! We were all mighty sick an' sorry to hear 'bout his son being lost thataway. There—I ain't introduced myself at all, have I? I'm Martha Pigot, Mrs. Martha Pigot. Jethro, he was my late, he took over this emporium (that's what they been a-calling this store for most fifty years now) from his dad. Then when Jethro up an' died, well, it was just up to me to carry it on. Though it's enough to fluster a body a mite now and then."

"And I'm Pearl Wade." Mother's smile was more like it had always been, warm and friendly. "This is Holly, who's our eldest."

Holly somehow smiled, knowing Mom wanted good manners now. She summoned up a voice from somewhere to say "How do you do?" Just as Mom always wanted her to.

"Crockett"—Mom nodded to Crock and he followed Holly's example—"and Judy, they're twins."

She always had to point that out to people, Holly believed, because they did not look alike at all. Crock was tall, taller than Holly by a whole inch now, something which he liked to keep reminding her about because she

9 ⁊

was a year older. But Judy was small and plump, looking younger than she was. However, she knew her manners, and though Holly could see she was shy, she spoke right up to Mrs. Pigot.

"Now this is what I call a right nice family." Mrs. Pigot beamed back at them all. "Nary chick nor child we had. But somehow we never missed them. The neighbor kids, they kinda make this a meeting place, so I see maybe more of 'em at times than their own kin do. Now you all just come back here—I got the heater turned on. This pesky weather is enough to chill you clean down to your bare bones.

"I've got me a pot of coffee a-perking away an' there's a good plate of Mame Symmes' gingerbread as she brought over this morning 'fore the clouds burst like to drown us. Mame, she prides herself on her gingerbread, she does. Always comes in with a big sheet pan of it when there's a church supper or the firehouse has their benefit fair."

So moments later, the Wades found themselves three on a bench, Mom on a chair, in a smaller room off the big cluttered store, each with a large piece of moist rich gingerbread in one hand, a mug in the other. Mom had coffee, but Mrs. Pigot had poured milk into the mugs the children held.

Crockett nudged Holly in the ribs. "This is not bad," he mumbled through a too-full mouth.

But Holly remained wary. Sure, Mrs. Pigot was friendly and made them feel welcome. But—what about this town? In Boston there had been others like themselves, they had never felt conspicuous because they were of another race. Here—it might be a different matter. And Mrs. Pigot had called Grandpa "old Lute," not "Mr. Wade." Somehow that disturbed her to remember. And—Mom *had* been different there at the very first, almost as if she expected Mrs. Pigot to be unfriendly. Holly wished Grandpa would hurry and come and they could get—no, no, she would not think of it as *home!* Now the gingerbread had no taste at all as she had to swallow it past a big lump in her throat.

"Quite a ride in from the old Dimsdale place." Mrs. Pigot did not sit down with them, but leaned against the side of the door and chattered on. "In this weather Lute might find himself having to take it slow. That old truck of his has to be humored a mite, I wouldn't wonder. You gonna stay at the junkyard long?"

Junkyard? Holly stopped chewing to stare at Mrs. Pigot. "Old Lute" and a *junkyard!*

"I'm going to be on the staff at Pine Mount," Mom was saying cheerfully. "The children will stay with their grandparents."

Mrs. Pigot nodded. "They'll find that a lot of young'uns in this town will envy 'em. Why, I don't know a boy hereabouts as doesn't like to go grubbing out there whenever he can get a chance. Treasures for young'uns, some of that trash is, or at least that's their way of seeing it. Was like that myself when I was their age. 'Course then it was just getting started, the dump. Lute and Mercy, they was just a young couple. Old Miss Elvery Dimsdale, she up an' died the second year they was working for her. Then it came about that there was a big tangle—legal that was —over who was to inherit, though there sure weren't much left.

"The big house, it burned down right before Miss Elvery died. She got touched in the head an' used to go wandering about at night. Never had no 'lectricity put in, so she'd take a lamp or a candle to see by. Well, she had a fall, an' Lute, he got her out. But the lamp she was carrying spilled out and the whole place—it was more'n two hundred years old—just went up in smoke! Folks started talking about the Dimsdale curse again, what with Miss Elvery getting so bad hurt that she died 'bout four months later an' the house going that way. She was the last of the Dimsdales, as far as the lawyers could make out, 'cept for a cousin off in California or some such place.

"Then they couldn't sell 'cause there was a flaw in the title, and the town didn't have no use for the land, 'cept as a dump. That's how the junkyard started—"

"What curse?" Crockett broke in, as Mrs. Pigot paused for breath.

"The witch curse, sonny, as was laid on all Dimsdales for almost as many years back as that old house stood. Story's so old now nobody can tell you the right of it, 'less Miss Sarah over at the library. She makes a hobby of looking up old town history an' might have found out something. There used to be witches hereabouts. Though they didn't have the hangings like they had over to Salem. But anyway there was a witch that the Dimsdales got across somehow, an' she laid a curse on them. Seems like they were a family mighty prone to ill luck in every direction. But some families are like that. Anyway they're all gone now, just like that house of theirs. An' Lute, he's a good man—an' Mercy, she's a good woman. They ain't been troubled none by something which was ended long 'fore any of us roundabouts was even born."

"A witch—with a gingerbread house?" Judy looked down at the small piece she still held in her hand as if it might have been broken off that dread dwelling, a picture of which was in her favorite fairy-tale book.

"Just a story," Holly said quickly, to show that she knew very well that witches and magic were only that. "People believed like that a long time ago, they don't anymore."

Mrs. Pigot was nodding again. "That's the truth— tongues will wagwag over nothing at all. They used to take a spite at some poor old soul as lived alone an' maybe had a cat to talk to. Then they'd call her witch an' make a mite of nasty trouble for her. Don't you fret none, honey, there ain't no witches at Dimsdale, only a lot of interestin' things, an' you're gonna like it right fine—"

As if her last words were a summons, the door of the store opened. Once more wind and rain came in with such force they seemed to propel with them a small man wearing a water-slicked raincoat and boots such as those which stood on the other side of the store.

He had a big yellow sou'wester hat, like those Holly knew fishermen wore, tied down on his head with a piece of cloth as if it were far too big and would be otherwise ripped away by the wind. And he fumbled with the knotting of this until he could pull it off and face them.

"Father Wade!" Mom was up, moving to meet him.

Daddy was a big, tall man, but Grandpa was hardly Mom's height. He was smiling, showing gaps in his teeth, but his voice was very deep as he answered, "Pearl, now ain't you jus' as pretty as yore name. Mercy has yore picture right up on the wall, but you is twice as pretty!"

He seemed surprised when Mom kissed his cheek. Then he caught her arms near her shoulders and brought her closer to him in a kind of half hug, as if he were afraid he might hurt her if he squeezed her too tight.

"An' th' young'uns." He swung about to see them,

still keeping hold of Mom as if he were afraid she might disappear. "Does my eyes good to see you, it certainly do!"

"Grandpa!" Judy had made up her mind at once. She ran toward him as she would have greeted Dad, her arms outstretched, and he caught her in a big hug. But he shook hands with Crockett, as if he knew very well that hugging was for girls and women, and with men it was different. Holly approached more reluctantly.

This small man, wearing a patched sweater and overalls under his old coat, he—well, she could not greet him as wholeheartedly as Judy did. He was still a stranger. But she kissed his cheek as Mom had done, and when he hugged her she did not resist. Though her nose wrinkled at the queer smell of his coat, and she felt more apart than ever from what had always been warm and secure.

There was a small truck waiting outside. Mom and Judy could crowd into its cab with Grandpa. But Holly and Crockett had to go in the back, pulling a piece of stained canvas over them. Holly looked out gloomily at the window lights of the store as they bumped away from what now seemed like the last outpost of civilization.

"Where do you suppose we'll live?" she asked Crock. "Mrs. Pigot said the house burned down—"

"There must have been another one," her brother returned carelessly. "Or else Grandpa built a new one. He's been living there, and Grandma. Dad was born there—"

"In a junkyard!" Holly exploded. "We're going to live in an old, dirty junkyard. Crock, I don't believe it! Mom couldn't have known about that—she won't let us—she won't let us stay—not there!"

"Wait until you see it." Crockett apparently was not

as concerned, but then boys didn't seem to worry so much about such things.

"We'll have to go to school here," she reminded him. "You want people knowing you live in a junkyard?"

"But Mrs. Pigot says the town kids like to come out to Dimsdale. They think it's fun."

"Maybe it would be," though Holly had doubts concerning that also, "if you didn't have to live in the middle of it. Mom just has to take us out of here—she's got to—" Her voice was raised. But she stopped short as Crock caught her wrist in a grip so tight it hurt.

He was looking straight at her and his eyes were fierce. "Holly Wade, you leave Mom alone. Don't you dare go whining at her now—you hear me!"

All the troubles which had ridden her for so long, ever since that hateful telegram had come, boiled up in Holly. She exerted all her strength and jerked free from his hold.

"You can't tell me what to do, Crockett Wade!"

"I can sure try if you make any trouble for Mom. She's had enough. You think you're so smart 'cause you get good grades in school an' are a year older than Judy 'n me. But you're dumb, Holly Wade, you're good and dumb when it comes to being helpful to Mom. You've done nothing but go around saying mean things and acting even meaner! Dad would be 'shamed of you, he sure would!"

Holly wanted to scream, to reach out and slap Crockett right across his big mouth. But that was being a baby—like being sick on the bus. She wouldn't let him know how bad he made her feel. She'd never let him know that. Deep inside she also knew that Mom would not take them away, no matter how hard she might beg. No, she would

have to be a new Holly Wade, one who lived in a junkyard, rode around in an old truck with a piece of dirty
old canvas to keep off the rain, stayed in a place where
a witch was supposed to have cursed a family—

Cursed a family—how would it feel to be a witch and,
as in the old fairy tales, have wishes which would come
true? Holly knew exactly what her first one would be:
that the telegram had never come, that they were back
in Boston with life going on exactly as it always had. If
she were a witch, that's what she would do with her
magic.

She continued to add to that dream as the truck turned
off the highway into a side lane and trees and brush
began to wall them in, adding to the darkness and gloom
of the day.

2 Treasure Trove

There *was* a house at Dimsdale, but such a queer one.
The Wades did not get much chance to see the outside
of it because they were hurried from the truck right in
through a side door. But once inside, Holly pushed off

her rain bonnet, which had hitched forward over her face like a mask with red flowers printed all over it, to see better.

There was one big room, darkish in the corners, for all the light came from a lamp set on a table. To one side an open stair went up steeply, but the room was divided in places by partitions which rose only to Holly's chin, if she tilted her head a little. These ran along one wall like a lot of wide cupboards without doors. They were full of things, as if someone had shoved furniture and boxes in as tight-packed as they would go. Two of them had shelves around the walls, and on those were what looked like piles of dishes, even a row of electric toasters set side by side. In some ways that very cluttered section of the room resembled Mrs. Pigot's store, except there was even less space to move between all the things which had been jammed in together.

At the side of the lamp table was a big fireplace, tne largest Holly had ever seen in her life. So huge was its cavern that there were even seats in the side walls, as if people could creep in there and warm their toes and hands at a fire kept burning in its center.

Smells—such strange smells—some spicy, some like cake baking, others Holly had no name for. But good smells, she decided, against her own desire to find every fault with the house in the junkyard. There was no one to greet them. Grandpa had taken the truck on to wherever his garage might be—but where was Grandma?

On the table beside the lamp, newspapers had been spread out to protect a red-and-white-checked tablecloth. On these were some broken dishes: cups without handles, plates cracked across.

Were Grandpa and Grandma so—so poor that these were the only sort of dishes they had? Holly was shocked out of her private misery to consider that. Before she dared whisper such a question to Mom, a door at the end of the very long room opened and Grandma came in.

Just as Grandpa was much smaller than Holly had expected, Grandma was taller. She was thin and walked bent forward a little, as if she were always so eager to get to where she was going that she would push her head well before the rest of her. Her hair was pulled up to a tight knot on the top of her head and in that were two combs with glittering stones set in them, one red, one green. On her nose was a pair of glasses, their rims bright red, curving up sharply at the sides. And they did not stay in place very well; she kept raising her hand to shove them back closer to her eyes. She had a sweater on, in spite of the room being so warm from the fire (plus a big stove on the far side of the table) that the Wades had loosened their coats and allowed them to slip off. But over most of this and a bright plaid skirt, she wore a big apron which had so many spots and stains of various colors spattered over it one could not be sure it had ever been white to begin with.

"Praise the Lord for His mercy. Here you are safe an' sound. An' it is good, yes, it's good, to see you, daughter!" She held out her arms to Mom, and Mom went right into them, as if she had wanted or needed nothing more than to have Grandma welcome her so.

"Good He is to us, child." Mom's head was hidden now on Grandma's shoulder. And Holly realized, with another stab of that queer fear, that Mom, the always strong one, was crying. "Good He is. Things come right in their own good time. So it has been for us. Many's the dark

19 &

hours we've had in the past, Luther an' me, but there is always somethin' the good Lord sends to be a comfort. I ain't believin' that Joel is dead. Don't you give heart-room, or head-room, to such thinkin' either! Joel, he's a fighter—he ain't going to be downed, not Joel!

"Now you sit down here." She led Mom over to a high-backed bench near the fire. "This is a day the Devil hisself might have sent to plague them what has to be out in it. Rest you, daughter, rest you an' be comforted. You are safely home—an' Joel will be, too. All in the Lord's good time."

Mom was smiling a little now, though there were still wet tracks on her cheeks. "You make me believe that, Mother Wade."

"Mercy—call me Mercy, daughter. It's more friendly-like here. Now—so here's the young'uns—" She gave a pat to Mom's shoulder and swung about to give a searching survey to the children, pushing back her glasses twice with a kind of thump as if she must have every bit of aid those could offer in order to make sure she would know her grandchildren the next time she laid eyes on them.

"Holly," she nodded, "an' Crockett, an' Judy—"

"Daddy calls me Bunny," Judy spoke up.

Grandma's face crinkled in a smile. "Does he now. Well, he was always a boy to go giving things names what weren't rightly their own. But somehow those names of his, they always fitted, anyhow. An', look now at that clock! Luther, he'll be wanting his vittles, an' so might you. Feeling a little peckish?"

Crock had been sniffing. "Something smells awfully good." He grinned back at Grandma. "You make gingerbread? That Mrs. Pigot down at the store—she gave us some."

"Mrs. Symmes' baking, I'll be bound." Grandma nodded briskly. "No gingerbread. But if you're like your daddy, you'll take a fancy to the heel of one of my new loaves— with honey-butter to liven it up a bit.

"Now"—she bore down on the table—"I'll just get my busy work out of here an' lay out for the full family of us." Though the dishes on the newspaper were all broken, she lifted them with care, carrying them to the end shelf in one of those queer cupboard rooms as if they were treasures.

"They're all broken," Judy commented frankly.

" 'Deed they are—that's why they ended up here." Grandma made a sweeping gesture to indicate the crammed small space between the wooden partitions. "But there's things which can be done for 'em. An' me, I do a right good job with a piece, if I do say so myself. All these things, they're salvage, you see. It's pure amazin' to see what people want to dump—pure amazin'! What's one folks' trash can be another man's treasure. Luther, he has fixin' hands—that's truly what you can call 'em— an' he puts together a smart lot of what comes in."

She swept around the table swiftly as she spoke, folding the newspapers on a pile by one of the cupboards, then going to a tall hutch against the wall and collecting more dishes, this time unbroken ones.

"Here, Holly." She summoned her elder granddaughter with one of those jerks of the head which unsettled her glasses again so they had to be thumped back into place. "You an' Judy can set table. Bowls for soup, the rest—"

Without question Holly found herself busy. Not one of

the bowls she set around matched the other. But they were not broken, and one or two were very pretty, with flowers and birds on them. The plates did not match either, nor did the forks and spoons and knives that Judy laid out with care. It was an odd-looking collection of china and flatware. Mom came over to watch them and took up one of the bowls, turned it over to look at the marking on the underside, and made a little gasping sound.

"Moth—Mercy—this is Minton!"

Grandma laughed. She was busy at the stove, pulling lids off pots bubbling there and sniffing the steam which arose from them as if she could tell from that alone whether the contents were ready to serve.

"That was one which came out just fine from my jigglin' around bits an' pieces. Can't tell with your eyes now, can you, that that came in broke near clean in half. Takes a lot of time an' patience. But, laws, I got time enough, an' patience is somethin' I need to learn, so I try my best. Here's Luther, now we can get down to eatin'. Which is something a body can do without any patience, just a good appetite."

While they ate Grandma's stew (she called it soup but it was far more like stew, Holly thought) and her newly baked bread (Injun bread, she told Mom—corn and rye baked all night in the old hearth oven with "just a taste" of molasses and such to give it flavor) with the herb jelly or honey to slop over it generously—while they ate, Grandma talked and they learned a lot about Dimsdale.

Grandma always called it that, and she didn't mention a junkyard. Instead she told about what lay outside, what was stored within the building which had once been a barn and was now their home, as if she and Grandpa were indeed keepers of a treasure house. Everything that was brought in to the dump was carefully sorted. Scrap metal went to a dealer in the city, who drove out three times a year. But the rest was Grandpa and Grandma's concern. All those things now jammed tightly into what had once been the stable stalls were things they were sure could be repaired.

"Lem Granger, he came back from Korea without his legs. But Lem was never one to let the bad luck get him down, no sirree!" Grandma slapped another plate of bread down to take the place of one which had been so quickly emptied. "He went to some school the veterans run an' learned how to repair electric things. When he gets a mite ahead of his repair work for other people, he comes up here an' takes a look around. Them toasters now"—she pointed with her chin to the row on the shelf, her hands being busy—"he'll look those over good. Likely he'll be able to take the whole kit an' caboodle an' fix 'em up to sell in his shop.

"The summer people, they don't want to fuss when something goes wrong, they just throw it out. Why, you'd be 'mazed, all of you, at what they pitch out when they bring in some of those big plastic trash bags jus' before they leave for back home in the fall. An' since they got that new lot of houses built across the Run—well, someone drives up from there three-four times a week with a bundle.

"Then there's the old families. Ain't many of them left now; when the last lone one dies they have a sale. What ain't sold, that comes here—an' we do get some strange things. There's a nice young man—his name's Correy—he an' his wife have started up one of these

23 ૭֍

here antique businesses down in th' old smithy. He comes up huntin' around. We keep a lotta the things from the old houses for him to see. He showed me about this china mendin', now he says that I can do it better than even the lady that taught him.

"We get in a mess of old books an' we call Miss Sarah Noyes who runs the library. The Scouts, they come out for the toy shop—you young'uns'll like a look around in there, I imagine. It's the furtherest stall that way. Starting 'long about now they get to work on toys, fixing 'em up, paintin' them an' the like. Most of those go out to the Blazedale Farm where the young'uns without families live. Luther—he's paid a little by the Selectmen for taking charge here. But, laws, we couldn't scrape along on that! We has our garden, an' the herbs, an' what we make outta sellin' what we sort out an' patch up. That's givin' us a real comfortable livin'. We're the lucky ones, I know that when I reads the papers an' all the news about what's happenin' around the world right now!"

Grandpa put his spoon down in a bowl so empty it looked newly washed. "Mercy, she's a great one for readin'—has a regular library herself of books she found an' took care of. An' she's always one for learnin' somethin' new—mostly what helps out, like this here dish mendin'!"

"Now, Luther, I ain't any more knowin' than you be your ownself. Ain't you fixed them tables an' chairs an' had Mr. Correy take 'em right away an' sell 'em first off? A hundred dollars he gives us for that table, an' ten apiece for the chairs, Luther did such a good job on them. An' the kin of old Appleby had thrown them out for broken bits only good for startin' a fire!"

It seemed that a junkyard was not quite what Holly

thought it might be. She was almost about to say that when Mom picked up the bowl she had said was "Minton" and began studying it closely.

"I can't see any mend at all, Mercy—it's like magic!"

"Magic, like witches do," Judy broke in then. "Grandma, did you ever see the witch—the one Mrs. Pigot said lived here a long time ago?"

Grandma's hand had been raised to send her glasses back into place again, but she never completed that gesture.

"Witch!" she repeated almost fiercely. "Them what has no work to keep them busy let their tongues wag a lot. There's no witches here, me'n Luther, we've been here a good forty years an' we ain't seen 'em. Witches were in the bad old days—they don't come botherin' people now. There were some tales about ol' Miss Elvery, 'cause she was one to keep herself to herself an' didn't take kindly to folks comin' in to see how she was doin'. (An' any time folks don't tell all they know an' throw open their doors to every Tom, Dick, and Harry, then they gets stories told 'bout them.) Miss Elvery was a good, God-fearin' woman as had mighty bad luck most of her born days—she weren't never no witch!"

The force of Grandma's voice silenced Judy. But Mrs. Pigot had not said that Miss Elvery was a witch, but that she—or her family—had been cursed by one. However, Holly decided, this was not the time to try to correct the story. It was too plain that Grandma did not want to talk about it.

In fact, she bustled about after their supper as if she wanted to see them all in bed and out from under her feet as soon as possible. And she fairly hurried them upstairs to show them what she explained had once been the coachman's quarters plus the old barn loft, but which had now been divided into small rooms, each of which was just about big enough to hold a bed, a chair, and a tall cabinet which Mom explained was called a wardrobe and which people used to hang their clothes in before closets were a regular part of the house. There was a washstand in each room, too—no bathroom. Holly regarded the basin and jug on the top of her and Judy's washstand with a return of rebellion. A house without a bathroom—having to wash in water you lugged upstairs and then probably down again. She was almost ready to explode but when she saw Mom's tired face, she remembered Crock's warning and did not spill out her sense of outrage.

She and Judy shared what must have been a larger room. It was shivery cold, so they undressed hastily and pulled on the warm pajamas Grandma had unpacked and laid out on the bed for them. There was a lamp on the top of a chest of drawers and Mom warned them not to touch it; she would come for it later.

"I like a junkyard," Judy said when they had finished their prayers and were settled under blankets which were old but soft. "I like Grandma and Grandpa, and I'm glad we came here."

Holly said nothing. She was listening, not to Judy's voice but to the wind, which sounded far closer in its howling up here than it did down by the fire. There were strange creaks and rustles, too. She supposed that was part of being such an old house—barn—because this one was well over a hundred years old, Grandpa had told them. But she did not want to be sleeping in an old barn—she wanted to be home in her own bed—in her own bed— Then, in spite of wind, creaks, and all the rest, Holly went to sleep.

Mom brought up a big copper jug of hot water in the morning and saw that they washed, but she told Holly that after today it would be her responsibility. Because Mom was leaving on the morning bus for Pine Mount. Holly tried to shove that out of her mind. She had known from the start that Mom would be away. But then that had been in the distance, a time she did not have to face. Now that time was here. She put on jeans and a sweater over her shirt, and then made her bed and helped Judy finish hers, hoping if she kept busy she wouldn't have any time to think about Mom's going.

There were quilts for spreads, and Holly thought, as she smoothed hers up over her pillow, that they brightened up the room as the lamp had done the night before. Outside the window it looked as gray and cold as if time had skipped forward two months very fast and it was already winter—even though there was no snow.

Downstairs Grandma stood by the stove, flipping pancakes over expertly.

"Nothin' like a soapstone griddle," she was telling Mom. "All them new things runnin' off'n 'lectricity—they's always breakin' up or down, or somethin'. You don't get no trouble with a griddle like this one, no sirree!"

The pancakes came away brown and just right. Grandma set them out along with a big glass bottle which had a slender handle to one side and a top cut to sparkle as if it were a diamond.

"That's real maple syrup," she told them. "No store-bought stuff with just a smidgen of flavorin' added to fool you. We get it straight from th' Hawkins' sugar bush.

Luther goes over to give him a hand with the all-night boilin' down."

There was no cereal or orange juice such as Holly always had—but bacon, and the pancakes, and a big glass of milk. Even with the thought of Mom's going nagging at her, she ate.

"No sense in your goin' off to school till Monday. Two days at the week's end won't hurt you to miss," Grandma continued. "Th' bus'll pick you up at the end of the lane Monday mornin'. Luther saw as how Jim Backus—he drives the bus—was told you would be here. But Luther, he's got a job in town today when he takes your mom in, an' you can ride along an' maybe give him a hand. They had a sale at th' Elkins' place last Saturday. My, seems like all the older families are a-goin' fast. Them Elkins', they helped to found this town, along with the Dimsdales an' the Pigots, the Noyeses an' the Oakeses. It's a mercy they ain't gonna tear down the house. Folks from outside bought it—gonna fix it up like it used to be. They got it listed as part of our history now.

"Anyway what they didn't want to keep in the way of furnishin' they sold, an' Luther, he's got the word to go up an' take the leavin's, so he can just do that today."

She was beaming at them as if this was a treat. Holly wanted to scowl but didn't quite dare. In spite of all Grandma had said last night about making things over and like that—this was a dump, a junkyard. And Grandpa rode around in an old beat-up truck to pick up stuff people threw out, like a garbage man back home. Now they were going to have to ride along with him—help out. And kids from school might see them. Holly squirmed, looking down at her syrup-puddled plate. She wished she hadn't eaten all that, now she felt a little sick.

"That's super!" Crock swallowed a last bite and then raised his voice to agree heartily that Grandma had good ideas about how to spend time.

Judy caught at Mom's sleeve. "I don't want you to go!" Her voice sounded shaky, just the way Holly was beginning to feel. Mom sat down on her chair again and put her arm about Judy, hugging her close.

"Now—a week goes awfully fast. Before you know it, I'll be back. I'll have a lot to tell you, and you'll have ever so much to tell me. Remember, you write it down in your diary and then you won't forget a single thing! And you can write letters, and I'll answer them. You can use my red pen and that paper Lucy gave you for your birthday—that with the kitten on it."

"Speakin' of kittens now—" Grandpa had gone out, now he stood in the doorway again. In his hand was a half-grown cat, its fur standing in wet points as if it had been in the rain for a long time. It lay limply in his hold, its eyes half closed. But as he brought it closer to the fire, it gave a small weak sound which was not quite a mew.

"They done it agin!" Grandpa handled the cat so gently, as if he were searching for some wound or a broken bone. The animal was shivering but it did not try to scratch him.

"I'll get th' basket, Luther. You hold him right there a mite to dry him off a little. I don't get my dander up much—most people have a reason to make 'em mean. But meanness to critters, that I can't abide, neither can Luther."

She had gone rummaging in the stall which held the shelves of broken china to bring out a large basket from which the topping handle had been broken long ago.

Into this she folded some of the newspaper from her work-table pile, and then she settled a faded cushion on top, poking it well down.

"People!" she said fiercely, snapping back her glasses twice, with such force Holly thought it might break the red frames. "They can be meaner than all them imps an' devils old Satan is supposed to have workin' for 'im. Because this is a dump, an' in the country—why, there's some as brings out poor animals as never done them any harm, an' jus' leaves them! We"—she glanced then at the children gathered around the cat basket to watch Grandpa settle the stranger in—"no, I ain't gonna say 'fore children some of the things we've seen. Now, Luther, you just set him down here an' I'll put out some warm milk—then we'll leave him be. If he don't come 'round by himself I'll fix up a doll bottle an' give it to him that-away."

"Can I pet him?" Judy had always wanted a kitten but Mom had said that in the city, with all the traffic on the streets, it was better not to get one.

"Not yet awhile." Grandpa had arranged his find on the cushion. "He's strange an' likely he thinks all the world's agin him. Rightly, after how he's been treated. You got to make friends slow-like. We'll leave him here where Mercy can keep an eye on him if he needs it. Maybe later he'll be willin' to trust us."

The rain had stopped by the time they left for town, but it was still very gray and cloudy. Holly and Crock shared a pile of bags for a seat in the back of the truck. Mom and Judy went up front again, with Mom's two suitcases back where they could watch them. Now that Holly had a better sight of the lane leading to the highway, she could catch glimpses, through thin places in the bush walls along it, of clutter which indeed made up a dump and a junkyard. The more she saw the less she liked.

They bumped up from the dirt and gravel lane onto the pavement of the road into town and went along seeing more and more houses. Some people had their lights on—the day was so dark. And the lights of Mrs. Pigot's store were bright as they pulled up before it.

Mom had her ticket, and the bus was supposed to be here soon. Holly hated to wait like this. You couldn't keep on saying "goodbye" and "remember this and that." You ran out of talk and then you began to hurt in your throat and you wanted to yell as loud as you could that Mom must stay, that you wanted to go back home and have everything as it was— She couldn't even look at Mom now.

It was good that they did not have to wait too long. The bus came to a stop. Grandpa and Crock took Mother's suitcases over for her. She kissed Holly and Judy and went across the road, to climb up the steps quickly, as if she could not say anything now either. Then the bus snorted and it was gone. Holly raised her hand and waved, though she was sure Mom could not see her, then let her arm fall.

"Freshenin' up a mite." Grandpa led them back to the dingy truck. "You young'uns get yourselves in the front now. Don't want none of you to turn to ice 'fore we get there an' back again."

Crock sat crammed in next to Grandpa, Judy perched on Holly's lap. Most of the outer world was hidden by her body, and Holly was glad. She had not cried, but it was a battle not to.

The truck swayed as it turned from one street to the

31 ❧

next, then it pulled into a driveway and around to the back of a big dark house. They scrambled out as Grandpa shut off the motor. Here was a stable barn, not as big as the one at Dimsdale. The doors of it were all shut and the windows boarded over. But at the side of the large door were some barrels and boxes, and with them a couple of old and very large trunks with broken hinges and many dents.

"Here we be," Grandpa said cheerfully. "Lucky nothin's too heavy to shift."

Crock was eager to get at that shifting, but Judy and Holly held back. Holly frankly did not want to touch the dusty, dirty stuff, and perhaps Judy felt the same. But with Grandpa looking as if he expected their help, the girls moved in.

It was when Holly found a much smaller trunk, behind the large one, and it broke out of her grasp (it was such an awkward thing to carry) that the pillow fell out on the ground. It was small (more a pillow for a baby, or maybe a large doll), and the slip which covered it was patterned all over with lines of stitching that did not even try to make a picture, but just ran round and round in broken circles. She picked it up hastily from the ground and a scent came from it, a strange smell which seemed—no, Holly was not quite sure what the smell made her think of. She tucked the pillow inside her windbreaker and the scent kept coming up into her face every time she moved. Such a queer thing—but, somehow, important. Why, she could not have told.

3 Tomkit and Dream Pillow

They had shoved the boxes and the two trunks into a shed, Grandpa saying that what these contained could be sorted later. From what she could see, Holly did not think there was much worth using. But both Crock and

Judy seemed to believe that there might be treasure hidden under the top layers of trash, Grandpa having told them stories all the way back from town about things which he had found from time to time.

"Folks," he announced, "don't rightly know what they've got sometimes. They want to clear out th' attic, or th' cellar quick so they just pitch out stuff without lookin' 'cause they say they ain't got th' time or nothin' good would be stuck away there nohow. Now you take that trunk—"

"It's all broken up," Holly said. With Judy on her lap, leaning back against her, the smell from the pillow stuffed inside her jacket seemed stronger than ever. She was still uncertain whether she liked it or not. And she began to wish she had tossed it back into one of the boxes before they had driven off.

"Yes, it sure is." Grandpa did not seem at all annoyed by her interruption. "But it can be fixed. An' nowadays some folks pay good money for them old trunks—paint 'em up pretty— Mr. Correy, he's sold three of them what we found, a couple lookin' even worse'n this to begin with. Th' Elkins, now they's an old family, been 'round here ever since there was a town—them an' th' Dimsdales. So we'll take care when we go over this here trash stuff—no tellin' what'll turn up."

"We can help, Grandpa?" Crock demanded.

"You sure can. Need some sharp young eyes."

Even Holly felt a stir of curiosity.

Then Grandpa continued: "We can't git to it today, nohow. Mrs. Dale, she's bringin' out some o' th' Cub Scouts this afternoon. They wants to go through th' toy shop—see what they can get fixed up for their fair next month. Always sell good at th' fair, an' then they'll pick out what can be made up as good as new again for the young'uns over to th' home."

So the trash, or treasure, from the Elkins place was stored in the shed, and they went back into the barn all very ready for the food Grandma was putting on the table. She had opened a small door set into the wall of the big fireplace to slide out, using a small shovel with a long handle, a big brown crock.

"Sure gives a man an appetite, Mercy"—Grandpa stood unwinding a very long scarf which went several times around his neck and then had the ends tucked in under his coat—"just to go sniffin' 'round in here."

"Beans an' pork," Grandma said briskly. "Fillin' enough. You get it all in one trip this time?"

"Yes. Seein' as how I had some good help to hand." Grandpa nodded at the children.

"Water an' soap waitin', over there." Grandma thumped her glasses into place and nodded at a bench to one side. There were three basins there and a dish with a queer lumpy bar of soap in it. A big can of water stood at the end.

Grandpa sloshed some of its contents into all three basins and beckoned. "Wash up it is, 'fore we git to Mercy's table."

Crock followed him over. Judy looked dubious, but obediently started for the bench. This was so different from running upstairs to the bathroom to wash at Mom's bidding. Holly again felt that need to be safely home where all was ordered and—right! She unfastened the zipper of her jacket and took it off slowly. As she did so the small pillow bumped out and fell, almost right in front of Grandma as she came with her quick steps to put a platter of sliced bread on the table.

Holly picked the cushion up. The scent from it was now almost too strong. And it did not feel like a regular pillow, rather as if it had been stuffed tight with bits of leaves, or grass.

"It fell out of a little old trunk when we were loading," Holly said quickly. "It's a pillow—I think—" Now, seeing it in the light, she almost doubted her first impression. It was too small for a bed pillow, surely, and not pretty enough to lie out on a divan or couch.

The material which covered it was coarse and yellow. And the embroidered lines on both sides ran around and around in circles which were broken here and there, as if some of the stitches had unraveled. Even if those lines had still been firm and complete, it would not have been a pretty design, not like the crewel-stitch pillows with ferns and flowers Mom had made last year.

Mom had made— Holly's hands tightened on the ugly little pillow. Her throat closed up and hurt again. Mom—who was gone with all the rest of that life which was safe and happy.

Grandma set the bread down on the table. Now she held out her hands, and Holly surrendered the pillow. She was glad to be rid of the dirty old thing. Grandma turned it around, looked carefully at the broken circles on either side, took her fingernail and pushed a little at the old stitches by one of those broken places in the circle. Then she raised it up to her face to take a long, long sniff.

"Lemon balm, costmary." She sniffed again. "Rose petals, mint—an' cloves an'—something else I can't rightly set name to." She favored the pillow with three more long sniffs. "No, me, I can't figure out that there last one. But with the rest—why, this here is an herb pillow, Holly, one made for them as can't sleep good at nights. Miss Elvery—now she had one she used when she had one of her headaches—showed me how to make 'em. For them you put in mints, an' bee balm, an' some orris root. But this is a sight more interestin'. That linen's real old, wouldn't surprise me none if it were hand wove, has th' look o' it. An' just about as good as th' day 'twas made, too." She squeezed the pillow energetically. "Insides might be gone all to powder. But this here"—she started tracing the design on the upper side with her finger and then stopped—"that do remind me of somethin'. Only I can't think jus' what at the minute. Laws, them beans is coolin' off. Go set this up with th' fixin's in the china stall, Holly. I'd like to think a bit more about this here—puts me in mind—only I can't remember what it puts me in mind of now."

Holly plumped the pillow down on a vacant portion of one of the shelves holding the broken china and washed in the basin. The soap, for all its strange appearance, smelled good—spicy. When she came to the table, Judy was pointing to an unusual thing made all of metal tubes cut off at one end but fastened to each other, open ends up, in a block. "What's that, Grandma?"

"That there's what earns me a bit of pin money, Judy. Mr. Correy, he lets me put out some things in his shop. An' I make herb candles in that. People like th' smell of them, it seems. That there mold, I'll wager it's nigh as old as this town. Now, Luther, will you say grace?"

Holly dutifully closed her eyes and listened to Grandpa's words about the food the good Lord had given them. He added something about Mom, and then about Daddy. She tried to shut her ears then, for fear she would be babyish enough to cry.

She took a big mouthful of the beans as quickly as she could. They *were* good, as good as the stew last night. Holly found she was hungry, after all.

"Grandma"—Judy spooned up the last mouthful of something Grandma called hasty pudding and served with maple syrup poured over it—"why don't you have any real lights, like we have at home?"

"Well, Miss Elvery—she didn't have no money to pay for 'em runnin' a line in when they brought the 'lectricity out this way. An' after she died an' the town took over Dimsdale, th' folks there weren't gonna pay for it. Selectmen, they don't pay out not a dime more'n they have to. Me an' Luther, we'd always used lamps an' such. It just come natural to us. Just like using well water an' some other things folks in town think is strange nowadays. My mammy, she was real poor, Judy. Only she was wishful for all of us to do better, an' we did. My brother, Jas, he went on the railroad an' did right well for hisself. Missy an' Ellie May, they went to th' big city, got themselves smart jobs workin' for families as 'preciated all they done.

"Me an' Luther, we done well, too. We ain't livin' off'n no relief an' we got us our own home place. Luther has hisself a good business here. Your daddy, he was always one as wanted to get ahead, too. He went clean through high school. Then he joined the army—said as how he was going to learn a lot there. 'Cause the recruitin' man told him as how there was chances to learn a trade, even if you did it while you were soljerin'. He got right good at what he was doin'—th' radio thing. Did so good"—

Grandma stopped a moment in her stacking of their pudding bowls—"done so good that th' Colonel hisself wanted him with him in Vietnam, said he knew he could depend on Joel. I guess Joel, he was kinda pleased to be goin', too—in some ways. He always had a hankerin' to see 'round th' world. Lawsy, how he used to get out all them old *National Geographic* magazines we fetched in when people came dumpin' an' jus' read and read. Got me an' Luther to readin' along with him.

"We never had much schoolin', you see. 'Cause we had work to do. Luther, his pappy died when he was jus' about Holly's age here, so he went to work then over to th' sawmill at Riverton. His mammy sure was able to use what he brought home. But he could read, an' figger, an' write —an' you can keep on learnin' if you're not lazy-minded. You come an' look here—"

She turned away from the table abruptly, beckoning so urgently that not only Judy, but Crock and Holly followed her away from the warmth of the fire-stove portion of the barn toward the more chilly space at the far end. Here were more shelves nailed to the portion of the last stall on the outer side. And these were crowded with books. Some looked badly battered, had even lost one cover or two. But they stood straight, and Grandma touched her fingers to the backs of the nearest ones gently.

"Library—we've got a library to our ownselves. Me an' Luther, we've read nigh every single one of these here. 'Course th' library truck comes around twice a month, down to th' Forks. But it ain't always easy to get down there, not in winter. Th' country men, they cleans off th' main road, but in winter th' lane's sometimes too snowed up to make it. But we ain't without books, even if we can't git down to the truck."

Crock inspected the shelves. "They're real old, some of them, aren't they?"

"Guess so. Miss Sarah, she takes those the library can use, but there's a lot left over. Magazines, too. So we got ourselves a library an' it's a good thing to pass th' time when it's winter an' we ain't got much business with th' junk. I found me a parcel o' books about herbs. Them I keep right to hand 'cause I try things they tell about— they being old an' sorta forgot in these days. There's some books for young'uns, too. But mind you, treat 'em right. Books should be real treasures, I always think. A lotta thinkin' an' hard work must go into writin' a book.

"Now then." She returned to the table. "Mrs. Dale is bringin' out those Cubs of hers after school, so we have to git everything smartened up a bit. Luther, you an' Crockett here, why don't you go an' see as how things back in the toy stall are loosened up a mite so as they can crawl around an' look at 'em good. We'll just clear way these here dishes—"

A little to her own surprise, Holly found herself with a dish towel made from an old sack in one hand, using it on the warm plates, mugs, and bowls that emerged from the big tin pan in which Grandma vigorously plunged them, while Judy took them when dry to stack on the proper shelf.

"Many hands make light work," Grandma said. "That's an old sayin' an' it is a true one. I'm glad Mrs. Dale is comin', gives you young'uns a chance to meet her. She teaches fifth grade at th' big school—"

"I'm in fifth grade," Judy broke in eagerly. "Will she be my teacher?"

"That she will. Now you, Holly, you'll probably have Mrs. Finch. She's a lot older'n Mrs. Dale. Some folks think she's strict. But she's fair an' she treats you right. Only she'll expect you to try hard—"

"Holly got an honor report card last time," Judy supplied. "Mom let her choose a prize and she chose going to the movies—all of us. We saw a Walt Disney, about Bambi. It was an old picture, but we'd never seen it before, only a little bit of it on the TV. It was good, all about a baby deer."

"Was it now? Well, come a little later you'll maybe get to see a real deer. Luther, he takes kindly to animals. He puts out hay when th' weather turns bad. Th' deer come in last year—"

"Grandma—" Judy turned to look at the hearth—"the kitten, what happened to the kitten?"

"He dried hisself off after he'd had a good feed. Then he went explorin', likely to turn up most anywheres about. Cats is like that, they is curious, want to know all about a place 'fore they settle in. There now—he might have known we was talkin' about him."

The gray cat appeared, as if he were a shadow able to detach himself from the other shadows, to sit before his very empty, well-polished plate on the hearth. When he saw that they were watching him, he opened his mouth as if he were mewing, only Holly could not hear a sound. Certainly he did not look as bedraggled as when Grandpa had brought him in. However, he was still so thin his bones stood out visibly under his fur.

"Eatin' time again?" Grandma shook her head, but she poured milk into his bowl and added crumbled dark bread. "Seems he has a likin' for bread—some cats have queer tastes that way."

"Are you going to keep him?" Holly wanted to know. The cat did not bear much resemblance to those in the

41 &

pictures of the cat books she had brought home from the library. She had always hoped that someday they could own a Siamese or a Persian. This cat looked like one of the half-starved prowlers they sometimes caught a glimpse of in the city.

"If he chooses to stay, he's welcome," Grandma said. "A cat chooses a home mostly, won't stay with folks he don't like nor in a place he don't take a fancy to. We'll see what he decides."

"What will you call him?" Judy wanted to know.

"Tomkit!" Holly was surprised at her own prompt answer. Tomkit—such a silly name! She couldn't remember ever having heard it before! Why had she said that?

"Tomkit," repeated Judy. "Oh, you mean like Tom Kitten, Mom used to read about—the one in the Roly-Poly Pudding story. I'd almost forgotten about him. 'Cause that was a book we had when we were very little."

"Tomkit," repeated Grandma thoughtfully. "All right, Tomkit he is."

The gray cat stopped gobbling down the contents of the bowl and looked up—straight at Holly, she was certain. Just as if he knew that name. Perhaps she had had it in mind from that long-ago storybook. Only somehow she doubted that. However, it seemed just right for this stray.

She and Judy helped Grandma, to "straighten up" the barn-house, as she put it. Then they went to see the things Grandpa and Crock were dragging out of the end stall. There were two bicycles, both pretty much wrecks; a wagon without a wheel, some stuffed toys, part of a train set. Most were so broken that Holly could not see much use for them. And she did not like getting into the mess. Finally she went and told Grandma she would write a letter to Mom, then climbed the stairs to find her paper and ball-point pen.

She had them in hand, and was ready to go down into the warmer section of the barn-house, when she heard noise below and guessed that Mrs. Dale and her Cub Scouts had arrived. They sounded as if they were all talking at once—about a hundred of them, or at least ten. Holly sat down on her bed. She did not want to go down, to meet all those strangers. Junkyard—what would they think of the Wades living in a junkyard, even helping to collect dirty old rubbish as they had this morning? This was a junkyard and they lived in an old barn full of junk —and—and—

She threw herself face down on the bed and bit hard at the quilt where it covered her pillow. No, she was not going to cry! But Mom! Now she did not want to write to Mom, she wanted to see her right here in this room— Mom coming to say it was all a mistake, they were going home and all would be just what it had been before.

"Holly?"

That was Judy. She did not even want to look at her. But if she didn't, then maybe Judy would go back and tell Grandma Holly was crying or something like that.

"What do you want?" she demanded fiercely.

"Holly, aren't you coming down? Grandma's giving us all doughnuts, and Mrs. Dale's so nice. Come on, Holly—"

She supposed she would have to go. But didn't Judy remember Mom at all? Didn't she want to be home again? Holly swung around on the bed.

If Judy had cleaned herself up before lunch, she was not very clean now. There was dust and something which looked like oil on the front of her shirt. One of her braids had come loose and flopped over her eyes. As she pushed the hair back impatiently, she left a very dark streak on her brown forehead.

"All right." Holly wanted to stay where she was. Only fear of what might happen with Grandma (who she was now sure missed seeing very little) got her to her feet, down the stairs, and brought her behind Judy, who was bubbling over with descriptions of what they had found and what could be done with it.

Mrs. Dale was pleasant, Holly had to admit, though she begrudged even that much of a surrender. The boys burrowing into the junk Grandpa and Crock had brought out said "Hello" in an offhand way, as if they did not really see her. But boys always acted like that. Holly was more noticing of one thing—they were all white.

What if there were no blacks in the new school? Would that make a difference? Who could Judy and she be friends with? She wasn't going to push in where she wasn't wanted. And she must see that Judy didn't either. All the time that she talked politely to Mrs. Dale, as Mom had taught her, Holly wondered and worried. She couldn't come right out and ask, somehow. Only how she wished there were some way of knowing.

The thought of the new school and what it might mean was in Holly's mind all during the weekend. On Sunday they went to church with Grandma and Grandpa, but that was not to a town church. They took a longer drive, over the river, to what had once been an old one-room schoolhouse. There were all Grandma and Grandpa's old friends, and most of them were old, also. There weren't too many of them, and the minister they called Brother Williams, he was really an old man. No children except some who weren't more than babies or others who were grown up—or thought they were. It seemed to Holly a very queer kind of church, and without Mom there—

In the afternoon, for want of something better to do, they explored Grandma's library. Sure enough, there were some old books supposed to be for children. Judy fastened on a Nancy Drew mystery that had lost one cover and had a lot of pages mended with Scotch tape. Crock found a pile of *National Geographics*. But Holly, feeling very dull and unhappy, pulled out books listlessly, glanced at them, and shoved them back on the shelves again. She finally discovered a very battered copy of what seemed to be six magazines bound together. The title on the stained red cover could hardly be read, but she made out the words "St. Nicholas." Inside, the pages were stained and mended, and the pictures were very queer. But it was very old because the date also appearing inside was 1895. She turned over the pages, trying not to tear them any more, until it was suppertime.

Monday morning they were up when it was still dark and had a chilly walk down to the lane's end, to wait there for the school bus. They waited so long that Holly began to hope the driver had forgotten their stop and they would have another day's reprieve.

But the bus came at last and they got in. The seats were crowded, there was nothing to do but push toward the back, facing all the strangers, who stared at them as they went. Crock saw one of the Cub Scouts, who hailed him, and he sat down there. But Judy and Holly had to go to the very end. Holly was sure her worst fears were proven true. There was not a single black child there.

"Judy." She caught at her sister's elbow, gave it a hard squeeze to ensure Judy was listening. "You be careful—"

"Careful about what, Holly?"

"Don't you see? These are all whites, they may not like us. Don't push, Judy, don't you look as if you want to be friends unless they're friendly first. You be good and careful. They—they may say things—"

"What kind of things?"

"Well, that we live in a dump, and we're different, things like that."

Some of the brightness faded from Judy's face. She looked anxious. "But that boy—he called to Crock to sit with him."

"It's different with boys," Holly told her. "Don't you give these white girls any reason to think they're better than we are—to laugh at us. Just be careful until you see how they're going to act."

"Holly, are you scared?"

That was one thing Holly was not going to admit to Judy, who was a whole year younger and sometimes quite childish.

"No. I just want to be careful. And you be careful, too."

"All right, Holly." Judy's voice was very low. She sat looking down at her school bag where it rested on her knees, Grandma's lunch making a big bump in the middle.

Holly was careful, very careful. She spoke when she was spoken to, but she made no advances. She did not volunteer in class, even when she knew the answers. And she did not try to join the other girls at recess or lunchtime, but hunted out Judy to stay with her. She went on being careful, waiting for someone to say "junkyard," or "black," or make some remark she could resent. The other girls, some of them, did talk at first, but when she herself did not make any effort to be friendly, they let her alone.

That suited her—just fine. She wasn't going to try to get in where she was not welcome.

There were only three other blacks in the whole school, and they were all in the lower grades. On Thursday, Judy looked unhappy when Holly hunted her at lunchtime.

"Debbie asked me to eat with her today," she said. "Debbie's nice. Why can't I go with Debbie, Holly?"

"Go on." Holly stood up, clutching her lunch bag. "Be with her, let them laugh at you behind your back if you want it that way, Judy Wade! I don't!"

"No, please, Holly." Judy caught at her jacket. "You stay. Debbie eats with Ruth and Betty, and I guess they don't really want me anyway."

But Holly was uncomfortable as they sat together, knowing that Judy was unhappy. Maybe this Debbie would be different—like the girls at home. Only—she found that she could not finish the mince tart which was at the bottom of her bag and gave it to Judy.

When they got home that night they found Tomkit in his favorite place on the hearth, but he was kneading his paws on that small pillow Holly had forgotten all about. She rescued it from him (though he growled at being deprived of something he had manifestly taken a liking for) and squeezed it a little. The scent seemed as strong as ever. Grandma said it was made for people who could not sleep. But what might it do about dreams?

Dreams! Last night she had had such a bad one, she had wakened up crying, and nearly frightened Judy into doing the same. Then Judy had confessed that she kept dreaming, too, about Mom and Daddy, and how they were lost someplace where she could not find them.

"Listen, Judy," Holly said now, "you remember what

47 ಠಿ

Grandma said about this pillow—that it made people sleep? Maybe it could keep away the bad dreams. Suppose, suppose we try it—"

"We can't both sleep on that one little pillow," Judy objected.

"Sure." Crock had come up behind them. "You can take chances for it."

Holly held the pillow tight against her. She wanted it so much, the need for it was so strong she longed to say right now that it was going to be hers. After all, she had really found it, hadn't she? But Crock was right, Daddy had always said "take chances."

As she waited for Crock to turn his back and get two unequal pieces of paper strips to pull out from between his fingers, Holly tried to understand why she wanted the pillow so fiercely. It was strange, but not frightening—rather as if the pillow not only belonged to her but was something she needed. Just as years and years ago, when she had not been able to go to bed without her Pooh Bear on the bed beside her.

"All right, you first, Judy." Crock swung around.

"You have three pieces." Holly was surprised.

"Sure, I got to see what all the fuss's about, don't I? You first, Judy," he repeated.

She hesitated for a long moment over her choice and then jerked free the middle strip. Holly took the one to her right, leaving the last to Crock. When they measured them—Judy had won.

Reluctantly Holly surrendered the pillow, thinking deep within herself that this was just one more thing which was not in the least fair.

4 The Maze Gate

There were no bad dreams that night, but Holly awoke early. The room she and Judy shared had only one small window, which did not let in much light. As she sat up in bed to glance over at Judy, she saw the long, furred body of Tomkit, stretched to the full extent of legs and tail. His face was next to Judy's, so they appeared to share the dream pillow between them. Now Holly could sniff that herb smell as if the pillow were able to scent the whole room.

"Judy!" Holly shivered, as she slipped from between her covers, put her toes into the furry slippers waiting by her bedside.

But Judy did not stir. Holly went over to her bed. Judy must be asleep. Yet now and then Holly was surprised to hear the faintest of murmurs. Her sister's lips moved, too, as if she were saying something, but in so low a whisper Holly could not make out the words, even when she leaned very close.

To Holly there was something frightening about that deep sleep and Judy's whispering.

"Judy!" This time she called louder, reached out to touch her sister's cheek, the one which did not rest against the old pillow.

She was answered first by a sharp hiss. A paw with the claws bared and ready for action struck out. Holly stared at Tomkit. He, at least, was awake. But, though he sat up, his eyes were slitted and his ears flattened back against his very small skull. He hissed again in warning.

"You old cat, you!" Holly exploded. "Get out!" She dared not raise her hand to push him off the bed, against his very open threat of retaliation. But she did seize the old pillow, to jerk it from under Judy's cheek, throw it away down the length of the bed.

Judy's head turned, her eyes opened. Only, when she looked up at Holly, there was something queer about her gaze. As if she did not see Holly at all, but someone else standing there beside her.

"Miss Tamar——" she said drowsily. Then she sat up, the quilt and blankets falling back. "The pillow—where's the pillow?" Catching sight of it where it had fallen near the foot of the bed, she scrambled out of the warm nest of her nighttime sleep to get it.

"Judy Wade." Holly was disturbed. "What is the matter with you?"

Her sister turned the pillow about in her hands, studying the broken circles on one side of it. She did not answer at once; instead she seemed entirely absorbed in tracing with a fingertip the lines of embroidery around and around until she reached the center of the circle. "Right there!" She nodded as if she were now entirely reassured of something. "We're going to find it right there!"

"Find what?" Holly demanded. "Something in the pillow?" She reached out to take it from Judy for a closer inspection, but the younger girl jerked it back and away.

"Me! I'm going to find it! 'Cause, Miss Tamar, she told me how——"

"Find what?" Holly's irritation grew. "Who's this Miss Tamar, anyway?"

"Find the treasure in the maze," Judy replied promptly, as if Holly were a little stupid not to know at once what she was talking about. "And Miss Tamar—she—she——" A frown began to gather on her face. "Holly, I don't know who Miss Tamar is. But she wants us to come, into the maze."

"What maze?" Holly was completely bewildered. What *was* a maze? She had a very vague idea that it was some kind of a puzzle. Suddenly she was sure she had a clue to Judy's strange behavior.

"You've been dreaming, Judy. You know what silly things happen in dreams."

Judy shook her head slowly. She was holding the pillow pressed flat against her now. "It wasn't a dream, Holly, it was all real. There is a maze and Miss Tamar wants us to come and see her. She showed me the way—every bit of it. We can go today. 'Cause it's Saturday! Mom's not coming today because of a special meeting, so we'll have time."

It was plain that Judy did believe her dream was real. Holly shrugged and began to dress. She knew better than to try to argue with Judy when her sister was in this mood. Usually Judy would listen to Holly's suggestions (which at times approached orders). But every now and then she got that certain look. When that appeared, Holly knew Judy could not be persuaded, or pushed, but would go only her own way.

This maze—it was certainly part of some very vivid dream. Judy would realize that for herself in time. However, as Holly pulled on her jeans, she kept glancing at Judy. Though Judy was dressing, too, she kept the pillow close beside her. Tomkit had moved forward to sniff at it with long, energetic sniffs, as if it were filled with catnip, though he did not extend a paw to touch it.

Holly wished that she had been the one to get the short strip of paper last night—had slept with the pillow. Judy was so excited about her dream. Could the herb pillow really make one's dream so real that it seemed to be true?

Now Holly did not try to talk Judy out of her belief that they were going treasure hunting in something called a "maze." When Judy could not find any such place, she would know she was just imagining it all. Making her bed smoothly, Holly decided that would be the only way to handle Judy, to let her see for herself that there was no maze, or treasure, or Miss Tamar. Tamar—that was a funny name, one she had never heard before. Where could Judy have picked it up to mix into her dream?

"I'm going to go down and help Grandma with breakfast," Holly announced abruptly when she had pulled on her tee shirt with the big red star sticker on the front.

"Okay." Judy did not even look up, or remind Holly that they usually spread their beds together. All she cared about now was that darned old pillow! All right, let the pillow help her then! Holly was decidedly cross as she stamped down the steep stairs.

Early as it was, Grandma was already busy at the stove. She had an egg mixture she was dripping into a skillet, stirring it around and around swiftly with one hand as she poured it out of a pitcher with the other.

"Good mornin', Holly. These here Saturdays are our busy days. Seems like everyone who has junk to dump comes in on Saturdays! Luther's got to be out bright an' early to see as how they don't dump it every which way. You can help, you young'uns."

Holly set out the mismatched plates on the table ready for Grandma's scrambled eggs. She did not just put milk in the mixture the way Mom did. No, Grandma added a pinch of this and a pinch of that from a row of bottles, each holding some dried-looking bits of leaves and things. However, Holly had her own problem of Judy's dream, and she wanted to make sure right from the start that her sister *had* been dreaming.

"You ever heard of a maze, Grandma?"

Grandma had reached for another small herb bottle. Now she did not unscrew its lid. Instead she swung around, to look at Holly as if, the girl thought, she had said someone was bringing in an elephant to dump.

"Now where ever did you hear tell of the maze, Holly?"

Could she say Judy had dreamed it? But Grandma would probably never believe her. And she couldn't lie, either. What was she going to answer?

"What is a maze, anyhow?" she compromised with another question, which was all that came into her mind at present.

"It's a garden thing they had in th' old days," Grandma said, as if she were thinking back a long way. "They planted out hedges in patterns on th' ground, with a door you could go in. Th' paths inside, between th' hedges, they ran every which way. But there was always a secret to it. An' if you made all th' right turns—then you got to th' middle. They say as how people got lost in 'em an' had to yell for help for someone to come an' show 'em th' way out. There was a maze here once. But all th' bushes grew up so big an' thick no one is ever goin' to get into that part of th' ground any more, 'lessen he rides in on a bulldozer. Most people have forgot all about it years ago. You hear about it at school?"

Again Holly evaded. "Judy heard." But she did not say that it was in a dream. Though she was near the big stove, Holly shivered. Why did Judy dream something about a maze which had really once been here? It was all the fault of that pillow—it must be! She should have left it lying back there in the Elkins' yard.

"Well, don't you young'uns go over hunting for it. It's all growed up an' thorned together. I would not swear that there ain't snakes livin' back in it. Sure looks nasty enough to give them house room."

Snakes! Again Holly shivered. And Judy wanted to go exploring there. Well, she, Holly, would get ahold of Crock, and they would both see that she did not.

She had wanted to ask about "Miss Tamar," also. If Judy's dream maze was real, then perhaps Miss Tamar could—but, no, that part *must* have been a dream, because Miss Tamar had told Judy to go into the maze. Holly set out the forks for scrambled eggs. If the maze was all grown together the way Grandma said, then she would not have to worry about Judy going in—there would be no way she could. But Holly promised herself she would make sure her sister did not try, not after Grandma's mentioning snakes!

Judy did not bring the pillow with her when she came downstairs. Grandma had had to call her just as Crock and Grandpa came in from doing what Grandpa called "makin' th' rounds." Which was really figuring out how to dispose of the trash in different places where it could be covered over by the 'dozer the town sent out once in a while. They had to be ready to see that the "Saturday dumpers" didn't just throw it any old where. Mostly the bigger pieces went into what had been the cellar of the house which had burned down years and years ago.

Of course, the trash had to be sorted, anything salvageable brought into one of the sheds or the barn-house. Just lately bottles, even the plates from TV dinners, could be collected and turned in for cash. So, as Crock informed his sisters rather loftily, it took a lot of looking to make sure you were not throwing away something worth good money.

He went out with Grandpa again when, just as they finished breakfast, a horn tooted. Grandpa said it must be the Larversons. They got the rent of a truck, now and then, to bring out all the trash for two streets in the new development.

Grandma, pouring steaming water for dishwashing

from an old teakettle so large it took both her hands to hold it steady, sniffed. "Trash is right—nothin' worth th' pickin' over."

"Well, it ain't old stuff," Grandpa agreed as he wound his long scarf on again. "But there's some good things for Lem once in a while. We'll always take a look-see."

When the dishes were done and Holly and Judy had straightened up their room, Grandma had waved them toward where their jackets hung on wall pegs. "You young'uns can get out an' leave me to my piecework." She smiled, and pushed back her glasses, as she started to spread out a layer of newspapers to cover the table-cloth. "Got me a real humdinger of a puzzle here, came in th' Elkins' batch of stuff. If I can jus' get it together rightly, Mr. Correy'll be more than a mite pleased." She had lifted an old pillowcase off her broken-china shelf and was unrolling its folds with care. Inside was a white statue, but it was broken. Holly, looking at it, did not see how anyone could ever fit those jagged pieces together again.

She picked up one bit which was part of a head, with the face. A bit of hair showed smoothly pulled back under what might have been the edge of a cap almost like the one Mom wore when she was on duty nursing, except this fitted down farther on the head.

"What do you suppose it is?" she wondered, being careful to lay the piece safely down on the cloth again.

"It's a woman," Grandma said confidently. "Maybe even a Rogers' figure. Them kind is worth a lot of money these days. They was like people out of stories, an' an artist man named Rogers, he made 'em. We'll just have to wait an' see if this one's worth fussing over."

"Holly, are you coming?" Judy was by the door, her

jacket on, her cap pulled carefully down over her hair. Between her feet, Tomkit wove back and forth as if he were just as eager and impatient to get going outside as she was.

Holly would have liked to stay and watch the magic Grandma might use to put together the badly smashed lady statue. But since Grandma herself had said for them to go, she guessed that such a job needed a lot of peace and quiet. Just wait until she got outside, she would tell Judy about the maze and the snakes—

"Come *on!*" Judy was out the door before Holly could pull on her cap. It was a chill morning. They could see their breath clearly, rising in white puffs. Judy's fairly exploded from between her lips, she was so impatient.

"Where?"

"The maze, of course!" Judy answered as if there could be no possible question about their destination.

Holly stopped short, caught at Judy's arm. "Now listen, we aren't going there. We can't get in anyway—no matter how you dreamed it—'cause I asked Grandma. She says it's all grown up wild, tight together. Besides, there's snakes in there. Grandma said that, too."

"Not if you go the right way!"

"What do you mean, the right way?"

"The way Miss Tamar showed me. There's nothing there to hurt you at all. And there's a treasure waiting—"

"Judy Wade." Holly took a firmer hold on her sister, who now squirmed to get away from her. "Now you know this is all a dream. There's no Miss Tamar—"

"Yeah?" Judy was certainly well into one of her very rare contrary spells. "You didn't even believe there was a maze, but now you know there is, just like Miss Tamar said. And I'm going there!"

She gave a stiff jerk and was free from Holly. With Tomkit bounding beside her, his gray tail in the air standing as a banner of triumph, Judy started to run toward the brown-gray mass of leaf-stripped bushes which made a wall of shadow some distance behind the barn-house. There was nothing Holly could do now but follow and hope to be able to reason with her when Judy did discover that there was no way into the entanglement Grandma had described.

"Hey, where're you going?" Crock came into sight.

"After Judy," Holly called as she went. "She's gone plain crazy."

He lengthened stride, was running with her now. "What you mean, crazy?"

"She—she thinks there's some kind of a treasure hidden back there." Holly waved at that not-too-distant wall of brush. "She had a dumb dream about it. Grandma says you can't get through, and there're snakes back there. We got to stop her, Crock."

"Snakes don't like cold," he said. "But what makes her think her dream is true? Judy's no little kid."

"Ask her!" exploded Holly angrily. "She just doesn't make sense. It's all the fault of that dumb pillow. She slept with it last night and now she thinks that somebody called 'Miss Tamar' told her how to get into a maze—Crock!"

Holly came to a stop, staring ahead. Of course this was as mixed up as that silly dream. But she *was* seeing it. Your eyes couldn't imagine things all by themselves—or could they?

There was Judy, all right. And she was not running anymore; she was standing still, her face turned toward them. She was smiling now and she waved to them to hurry. But it was not Judy which was so astounding; it was those—*things* on either side of her, like the posts of a door which had no top at all.

The brush which had seemed such a dull brown-gray when Holly had started away from the barn-house was not the same now she had come this close. Instead the bushes did have leaves, shiny dark green ones. And two of those bushes, standing much taller than Judy, had been clipped in a queer way to look just like—cats! Big green cats sitting up with their tail tips covering their paws, their faces much like Tomkit's.

Tomkit had settled at Judy's feet in exactly the same pose. His eyes were large and yellow-green; someone might have used him for the model when those hedge cats had been made. Now he got up, stretched his front legs, and went on, past Judy, past the cats, into the brush-walled way they guarded.

"Come on!" Judy again waved vigorously toward Holly and Crockett, was gone before Holly could stop her, or even call. And, once she had passed between the guardian green cats, they could not see her at all.

"Crock, we've got to get her out!" Holly began to run again. She remembered Grandma saying people could be lost in a maze—what if they could not find Judy? She was so frightened now that her heart pounded hard.

Then the green cats were on either side and she passed them, Crock right behind her. This was a green tunnel, for the bushes were so tall their uppermost branches met above in a loose woven roof. At their roots were other plants, less tall, but also as vividly green. As if this was summer instead of fall. The scent of their small purple flowers was strong.

Underfoot was a pavement of very old gray stones. In

all the crevices around these were small plants, which, when the children stepped on them, gave forth a very spicy smell. They caught sight of Judy again just a little ahead, where there was a forking of the tunnel-like way. She was shifting from one foot to the other and waving them on.

"Hurry! And you've got to follow me," she burst out before they joined her. "I know the way—the right way! Just as Miss Tamar showed it to me. It's this one—"

She turned right at the fork to enter another stretch of tunnel. It was growing warmer. Holly jerked open the zipper on her jacket, pulled off her cap to stuff it into her pocket. Why, it felt like summer now. There were other plants among those with the purplish spikes of flowers: some flowered, some with differently shaped leaves. When the children brushed past, each seemed to loose a new scent at the lightest touch of coat edge or sleeve.

The three came to another forking, and here again sat a tall cat clipped from the hedge. But of Tomkit there was no sign. He must have traveled far faster than they were going, for they were now slowed to a walk. It was very quiet in the maze tunnels, but the warmth, the scents of plants and flowers somehow quieted Holly's fears. She found herself looking more closely at the plants, none of which she knew. Though she did see what she thought was an odd-looking, cramped-up little rose, its petals all squeezed together, twining in and out among the hedge plants at one place.

Judy led them confidently onward, always to the right when there was a choice of ways. Holly had lost all sense of direction, and, though she thought that they might indeed be circling inward as the lines on the pillow top had gone, yet she could not even be sure of that.

Twice more they passed tall hedge cats, each facing in upon the way. However, there was nothing in the least frightening about them. Crock got as close as he could to the last, trying to figure out how the hedge itself had been trained to grow, or had been clipped, to make that living green figure.

They had all shed their jackets now, slinging them over their shoulders. For, while they could not see much of the sky overhead, a summer sun surely hung there. Holly paused to push up the long sleeves of her tee shirt. But Judy plodded steadily ahead as if she were on some very important errand.

The maze tunnel took a sharp turn, bringing them into the open. Holly blinked. Where—how—? She stared at what lay ahead of them now, and could only believe that somehow this was after all a dream, one which had begun realistically enough with the events of the morning and then turned into a kind of fairy tale.

Before them was an elaborate garden. But such a garden as Holly had never seen, even pictured in a book. Immediately ahead their path led straight into its heart. Plants and flowers grew in carefully measured clumps, some beds round, some narrow, some curved in half circles. Each bed held a different plant. However, the path itself cut straight across the garden, except in the very center, where it ringed around a pool.

Beyond the garden (which bore a likeness to Grandma's quilt with its precisely shaped pieces here being the different colored plants and flowers rather than cotton bits), was a house.

It was much smaller than the barn. And it had an odd appearance as if it had not really been made by men, but had somehow grown out of the ground. The roof had wide shingles, which were gray but patterned with a growth of green moss. And the boards that covered the outside walls were unpainted also, green-moss grown, running up and down, instead of crossways as in most of the frame houses Holly had ever seen.

A very large chimney of rough stones stood in the middle of the house. Small ferns grew between its cobbles here and there. The windows were small and quite high in the walls, while their panes were cut as glass diamonds fitted into dark metal strips. To one side of the house was the round top of a well. And, farther beyond that, a bench on which there were straw-covered, cone-shaped hives from which bees came and went.

The big front door stood open, and on the doorstep sat either Tomkit or his twin brother busily washing a hind paw, looking entirely at home.

Judy moved forward, down the path which led around the pool straight for the house. Holly thought she could see a faint trail of smoke curling upward from that very large chimney. It was plain someone lived here. The garden was very well tended, there were the bees—but who— And why didn't Grandma know or tell them about this near neighbor?

"I don't get it." Crock threw his jacket on the ground. "I just don't get it! This is summer, not October! And who—"

Crock was right. It was summer, only Holly refused to admit it. She did not dare think what *that* might mean. This was a dream, it had to be a dream! She closed her eyes—she'd just be waking up in the barn-house.

But when she opened her eyes, it was to see Judy almost through the garden and nearing the door. Suddenly it seemed to Holly that that door was waiting—maybe waiting to catch them—like a trap.

"Judy!" she screamed at the top of her voice, beginning to run again. "Judy, don't!"

Judy never turned or looked, nor did she pause. She was going right on! If Holly could not stop her in time, she was going right on into the house.

"Judy!"

Holly rounded the side of the pool. Here, in this quilt-garden, the flowers and spice smells were even stronger. Only she had no time to look, she had to stop Judy or something would happen. What that something might be she could not tell, but she was afraid of it, so much afraid.

Tomkit sat up in the same position that the green hedge cats had taken. He had the solemn look of one who was waiting—

Holly put on a last desperate burst of speed. She caught at Judy's shoulder.

"No, Judy!"

"But there be nothing here to affright thee, child."

Judy had not said that, spoken in those queer-sounding words. The voice had surely come out of the house beyond.

ಕ TAMAR

Holly still held on to Judy with a firm grip.

"Don't you go in there, don't you dare!" she cried fiercely.

Judy tugged and pushed to free herself. "What's the

matter with you, Holly? All the time we've been here you've been saying don't do this, don't do that. I'm getting tired of you telling me what to do. Now you just let go of me, do you hear?" Placid Judy rarely flared up like this. A last thrust freed her arm, and she marched straight into the shadowed interior of the queer-looking house, as if that were as safe as the barn, and Grandma were waiting with lunch for them inside.

For a moment or so Holly was so surprised at Judy's rebellion that she did not move. Then she saw Crock also on his way to the door.

"Crock!"

"What?" He hardly turned his head at all. "You know, Holly, Judy's got it right. You think you know it all, but you don't. You sure don't!" With this parting shot he vanished after Judy.

Around Holly the gentle breeze of summer curled, bringing with it heavy scents from the garden. There was the hum of bees. It was all so peaceful, welcoming—yet something far inside her was wary, uneasy. This simply was not real! She knew that early October was fall, and cold. There were no flowers left, not outside the green walls through which Judy had led them. And this house —Grandma, Grandpa had never said a word about it. The old Dimsdale house had burned down a long time ago. So this could not be that one. Who did live here? And why had Judy dreamed a way to this very door?

Holly could not pretend to herself now that this was still a dream *she* was having. No, it was something else, but strange and not right, and she was afraid. Judy and Crock, they had gone in—she would have to go too—she had to.

Reluctantly she went, step by slow step. There was a

kind of perfume in the air coming out of the doorway, meeting her full face as she entered.

Within seemed all one large room, with a huge fireplace, almost as big as the one in the barn-house, facing her. There were two fires burning in it, one at either end, and over each swung pots supported by chains which appeared to hang right down the chimney. A woman stood by one of the pots, stirring its contents with a slow, even turn of a very long handled spoon. She glanced up at Holly and smiled, and then went back to watching the bubbling liquid in the pot, as if that was a task which required close attention and care.

The big room was none too light, though some sunshine came through the windows at the other end. Also it was very crowded with a number of things Holly could not sort out at first. The woman herself held her full attention.

The stranger was perhaps as tall as Mom, but as to looking like Mom, or any other lady Holly knew—no! Holly shook her head to deny what she was seeing. Because that woman stirring the pot—she could *not* be real. Unless she was dressing up for some reason.

Last year, when Mom had taken them to see Williamsburg, there were ladies there who showed people through the old houses. And they all wore old-time dresses to match the houses they were guides in. Perhaps this woman was playing at being a part of the old times in the same way.

She had her dark hair all pulled back tight with a white cap over it, shaped like Mom's nurse's cap, only one which fitted much farther down over her head, to hide most of her hair. Her skirts (there were two of them, the upper one caught up on both sides to show a lower one) were very long and full. The lower one was a kind of yellow-white, and the upper one very dark blue. Above these she wore a long apron of the same yellow-white as the underskirt, and her bodice fitted tightly and was laced down the front. Around her shoulders was another piece of whiter cloth, like her cap, which was cut as a very wide collar and fastened up tightly to her throat.

Holly remembered where she had seen just such a dress before—in her history book. The woman was dressed like the Pilgrims in the scene of the first Thanksgiving. Yet she did not seem conscious she was wearing a costume at all, rather as if this dress were the only right one.

Since she had not spoken again or given any sign she knew the children were here, except to smile welcomingly at Holly, Holly studied the room. It was certainly overfull of things. Now that her eyes had adjusted better to the lack of strong light, she was able to see details.

Back against the walls were chests, very heavy and solid looking. Above those were cupboards. There was a long table in the center of the room, against which Crock and Judy now leaned their backs, as they watched intently the woman at her slow, careful stirring of the pot. On this were bowls and pots, a number of things all in disorder. And, alongside the table on the door side, was a bench. There was one tall-backed chair, and on that sat Tomkit, his eyes half closed as if he were about to go off into a nap.

By the fireplace stood a high-backed, longer seat, also two stools on which sat a jug, and several pots, with long-handled spoons and a couple of burnished copper ladles. And from the big beams overhead swung bunches of dried plants strung up by their stems.

Holly had gotten only that far in her survey of the room when the woman began to sing, quietly as if to herself:

> "Lavender's blue, dilly, dilly!
> Lavender's green.
> When I am king, dilly, dilly!
> Thou shalt be queen.
> Who told you so, dilly, dilly!
> Who told you so;
> Twas my own heart, dilly, dilly!
> That told me so."

From that old rhyme she swung into another:

> "The hart he loves the high wood,
> The hare, she loves the hill;
> The knight he loves his bright sword.
> The lady—loves her will!"

Then she laughed happily. Suddenly Holly found she herself was smiling. She did not understand why, but she had lost, for the moment, all that unhappiness which had been a sore place in her since the telegram had come. Tomkit had curled around and gone to sleep on the big chair. And Judy and Crock were smiling, too.

"Now"—the woman moved quickly, reached out a pair of tongs to take the pot handle in a firm hold and swing the pot itself off the chain hook and onto the flat rock of the hearthstone.

"Done well, no ill"—she looked down into the depths of the still-bubbling liquid within it. "It shall cool, then thee shall see—but I must make amends for such a sorry greeting. Blessed be!"

She raised her hand to make a little gesture toward them. She might have been counting them, one, two, three. A strange look at each, Holly thought; it was not as if she looked *at* them, but *into* them. For Judy and Crock she had a smile, but when she came to Holly, that smile faded a little and Holly drew back a step. She felt as if she had done something wrong. However, her uneasiness lasted for only a second. Once more the woman was smiling—or rather, the girl was—

The odd dress and that cap over her pulled-tight hair made her look older than she was, Holly thought. Her skin was tanned as if she were out in the sun a lot, and she was not pretty. Her chin came to a too-sharp point, and her nose was somehow too long. However, when she smiled at you, you forgot all that.

"You are Miss Tamar," Judy spoke.

"I be Tamar," the girl nodded. "Though there be others hereabouts as have other names for me. Thou art?"

"I'm Judy Wade," Judy replied promptly. "This is my brother Crock—Crockett. We're really twins, but nobody ever knows till we tell them. And that's my sister, Holly. We've just come to live at Dimsdale."

"Dimsdale," repeated Tamar. Now her smile was gone. "Aye, I be forgetting once again. That be not the Dimsdale that was, but the Dimsdale which *is* which thee knows. Still lies the shadow." She shook her head regretfully. "Still lies the cruel shadow—"

At last Holly found courage to speak up. "Where is this—this house? Grandma and Grandpa, they never told us about it, or you!" She wondered if she had spoken rudely, because Crock was glaring at her.

"This house be where it has always been," Tamar answered, but not with the facts that Holly felt she desperately needed to know. "It was, is, and will be—for it be of the earth and gifts of the earth."

Now she was smiling once again. "Ah, 'tis good to have

young faces here and guests beneath this roof yet once again. Aye, be that not, Tomkit?" She spoke to the cat as if she expected him to answer. But he only opened his eyes and looked at her sleepily.

"Is Tomkit yours?" Judy wanted to know. "Grandpa found him on the dump, he thought somebody had thrown him there."

"Tomkit be his own puss, he goes where he lists, does what needs to be done," Tamar replied. "Aye, child, no one may own a puss. It be his choice to live under thy roof, or another's. Tomkit I know, and he knows me. But never do I say Tomkit be mine to use as I will, for he hath a life of his own, and no man, or woman, or child, may own any life but his own. That be the Law.

"Does not that Law say plainly: 'That thou lovest all things in nature. That thou shalt suffer no person to be harmed by thy hands or in thy mind. That thou walkest humbly in the ways of men and the ways of the gods. Contentment thou shalt at last learn through suffering, and from long patient years, and from nobility of mind and service. For the wise never grow old.'" She said those words solemnly, like the grace Grandpa said at meals.

After a moment she ended: "So mote it be."

Those last four words echoed queerly through the room, almost as if they had been repeated very softly by other people. Yet none of the Wades had done so, and certainly Tomkit could not.

"There must lie truth within the heart," Tamar said, as she reached again for the cooling pot and lifted it to stand on its three stumpy legs on the table, "lest thy every effort be doomed to failure. And there be truth in this syrup—that will I take book-oath upon."

She worked swiftly, lining up a half-dozen small, dull

clay jars, and into each she measured by ladlesful the contents of the pot. It was from the thickened syrup that the perfume-sweet smell came.

"What is it?" Judy wanted to know. "That smells like perfume and like something good to eat both together."

Tamar did not answer at once; it seemed she was deeply intent on the exact measurement of each of those ladlesful that went into the jars. Then she dropped the ladle with a clang into the now-empty pot and gave a sigh of relief.

" 'Tis done, and well done! What be it, thou asketh, child? It be a syrup of roses, which in turn may be used in many different ways: in sweetmeats for the eating, in cookery, in the making of that to sooth ills away. It hath angelica in it also, and that be sovereign against the ills of the spirit. For sometimes it be true that the ills of the spirit lie harsher on mankind than do the ills of that flesh which he weareth for so short a span of years."

Holly listened carefully, but she was not quite sure she understood. Tamar spoke her words oddly, accenting some of them as if they were not the language Holly knew but that of another country.

"Those are all herbs"—Judy swept her hand up to gesture to the bunches hanging from the ceiling. "Grandma has some hanging up that way in the shed, but she hasn't nearly as many of them."

"Thy granny hath the lore?" Tamar said. "She be a wise woman then, and that be why thou hast had the way opened to thee. Aye, those be all which the good earth gives to us for heal-craft and the comfort of our kind." Her voice then fell into a sing-song, though she did not make it rhyme: "Mints, and bee balm, costmary, lavender, marigolds for sprains and wounds and their knitting;

71 ❧

pennyroyal that will make stagnant waters fresher, and which sailors do cherish for that reason; cowslips for wine to warm the stomach; basil, thyme, and rosemary, rue, meadowsweet, the red yarrow and the white, sage, purslane, pimpernel—aye, all those and full half a hundred more, past my naming lest I were to sit half the day a-doing it.

"Ground they may be, or boiled, set in dishes to give food a toothsome flavor, made into sweetmeats, and wines . . . Ah"—she threw out her hands as if to gather all about her into her grasp, her face alight and eager as Grandma's had been when she spoke of the mending of her china bits—"there be so much in this wide world that one can never come to the end of learning. And the goodness of the earth giveth all such richness beyond the thinking of men, who take ever and say not thanks. For they will not believe in the truth—that man must be one with that which grows, and that which runs, even the four-footed, and that which spread its wings and makes a home place of the sky. Men slay without thought, dig and tear without feeling, cherish not the great, good gifts. Beware should they be, lest all this be at last reft from them.

"However, these be solemn thoughts and not for guesting. Guesting be a time for feasting and making merry. Come, sit thee down and let us share together bread and wine, after the manner of good friends and folk-kin."

As she spoke, Tamar gathered up many of the things which were crowded on the long table, setting them elsewhere to clear a space. Judy moved to help her and picked up a box to set it away. But, before she put it down at the other end of the table, she bent her head to take a deep sniff.

"Please—what are these beads? They smell so good. Look, Holly—"

She turned the box so Holly could see that it was indeed half-full of red-brown beads. Some had been strung on thread and others rolled about loose. The scent of roses clung to the box.

"Ah, those," said Tamar. "They be a pleasant fairing—something for maids to have for the wearing. Though there be those who turn their faces upon any matter of such, and say that to use them so be a sinful flaunting. Those be rose beads. Thee must gather the flowers when they be fullest, and take the petals to put together in a mortar and grind well, into a paste. This thou rollest into a bead and leave it to dry. It be one, then, such as this, which be also fashioned to lay amongst one's linens, giving them a pleasant smell." She plucked out of a cupboard behind her a round brown ball which smelled of spice, a far more penetrating odor than the delicate one of the rose beads.

"For this thee takes a firm apple or, if there be such to hand, an orange out of Spain. In it thee sets stick cloves so tightly together that no bit of skin may afterward be seen. The fruit dies not, but gives rather this good smell for a long time thereafter."

Holly was entranced. She cuddled the knobby ball in her hands, smelling at it. Just as Judy continued to sniff at the box of rose beads. But Crock was edging slowly along the table, looking very curiously at all the jars, boxes, small scales, pans, and such, laid out to crowd now even more one end as Tamar cleared the other.

"You make these to sell?" he asked.

"Some. Some for my pleasure." She was setting out three plates of metal, a dull-looking metal as if it were

73 ॐ

silver which had not been properly burnished. "There is more healing in what grows out there in my garden than in any doctor's case."

"Grandma makes herb candles," he volunteered. "She sells them down at the antique shop. I bet Grandpa would like to see these." Crock was regarding a series of small boxes, each carved from wood. They were all lidded, but the knobby handle on each lid had been made in the likeness of either a leaf or a flower. "These are sure great; Grandpa carves too."

Tamar had gone to the farther end of the room and was returning with a big brown pot. She glanced at the boxes and then away—almost, Holly thought, as if something about them did not please her. Or maybe Crock was being too pushy—

"Aye, lad, there be many a man able with his knife and a bit of wood. 'Tis a goodly thing to make something of use, goodlier when one makes it also as a thing which be a pleasure to the eye. But that last be not the belief that many hereabouts hold in favor."

"I liked that—" Crock continued, far more talkative than he was at home. "What you said about loving things in nature, not harming with hands or what's in your mind. Grandpa, he thinks that way, too. He tries to make them cover up the worst of the dump, truly he does. And back a'ways he's planting trees—"

"Trees!" Tamar was watching the boy intently. "What manner of trees?"

"Well, little pines and a willow, things he can transplant from where they're bulldozing for the big highway on the other side of town. He showed me some. And he plants acorns." Crock grinned. " 'Course he said those would take a long time starting—"

"Oak, aye." Tamar nodded. "Oak be of the old ones, very strong in power. But ash he should have also, and elder. Elder be the mightiest shield against the dark. . . . And your granny?" She looked now to Judy, speaking with a hint of sharpness in her voice. "Does she also plant?"

"I—I guess so. She's got all these herbs she uses, she must get them from a garden somewhere."

"Aye, she plants. Then thee must also. For the good, be it strong enough, will drive out the ill. I shall give thee that which will be sovereign remedy: basil, mallow, hawthorne, hellesbore—"

"But," Holly spoke up, "we can't plant now—back there—" She was no longer sure just where the barn-house was. "It's cold—fall. They wouldn't grow now."

Tamar's eyes caught hers and held so for a long moment. Holly wanted to look down, away, but found she could not. Again there was that strange expression on Tamar's face as if she were not seeing Holly at all, the girl thought, but *through* her. That was such a queer idea that it made Holly so uneasy again she wanted to run away from the old house, back through the maze to safety.

Once more Tamar nodded, slowly. "So that be the way of it—" But she was speaking more to herself, Holly was sure, than to them. "Time doth twist and turn, coil upon coil, as lies the serpent in its lair." She might have been quoting some odd, ancient saying. Then that strange, through-Holly look vanished. "Welladay, seeds thou shalt have, and the roots—There are ways—ask thy good granny. A wise woman knows. Now sit thee down and break thy fast. 'Tis but little, hoe cake and bees' harvest, with cider."

75 ॐ

They slipped onto the long bench on one side of the table and tasted the crumbling rounds Tamar set out on their plates, she having spooned a generous gob of strained honey onto each. Into small tankards she poured from a tall jug, then stood watching them and smiling.

"What do you make besides rose beads?" Judy asked.

"What do I make? Ah, a half day's telling would not be the end of it!" Tamar laughed. "There be the healing powders and ointments, and those small things to bring taste to a dish. There be tussy-mussy for a lad to give to his lass—"

"Tussy-mussy?" Judy interrupted. "That sounds funny."

"It be a fairing, see? Each flower and leaf, they hath meaning for the knowing, also a scent which is mainly flavorsome. If such be fashioned of herbs, one takes nine kinds—a sprig, or a leaf—and binds it fast. If it be of flowers, now, then one bethinks the message for it to carry. The lad, he leaves it on the doorstep of a morning, and if the lass would favor him, she will wear it in her kerchief. Though there be those who frown upon such fancies, calling them idle and only for the light-minded."

Tamar sighed suddenly. "Aye, to those who seek for dark thoughts and hard ways, such be easy to find. They would even cloud the sun, lest it shine too brightly. They will not believe that there be good also in light and laughter. And—"

> *"Lavender's blue, dilly dilly!*
> *Lavender's green—"*

The same song Tamar had sung, but this was a man's voice and from outside the house. Tamar stood very still for an instant. It seemed to Holly that she looked frightened, or else very troubled, during that same instant.

Then it was as if she braced herself to face something difficult to do. Holly had seen Mom look like that; she had on that day she had shown their house to the people who were going to rent it.

Tamar's finger went to her lips as she looked down again at the children. They understood and nodded in agreement. Then she was on her way swiftly to the door.

Holly slid from the bench. She did not know who was singing outside, but she was determined to find out. Judy tried to catch at her sleeve as she slipped past. But she avoided that clutch and stole to the window, where she could just see above the sill.

Tamar was out of the door now. And there was a man, a young man, coming through the path of the herb garden toward her.

He had on leather breeches which only came below his knees, with thick stockings and big shoes with buckles on them. His shirt was white and had full sleeves gathered to tight bands about his wrists, and a wide, open collar. And his hair was long, reaching to brush his shoulders. It was black hair, and his face was brownly tanned. In his hands was a packet of leaves tied with grasses. And there was a smile on his face, though that faded as he faced Tamar.

"Good morrow, Mistress Tamar."

"Good morrow, Master Elkins." Tamar did not sound at all welcoming, and she was not smiling. Nor was he now. He kept looking beyond Tamar's shoulder at the house, as if he expected someone else to be there.

"*Master* Elkins," he repeated. "Are we then such unfriends, Mistress?"

"Master Elkins, well doth thee know that between us there can be no friends nor unfriends. Would thee bring

77 ᕫ∾

ill fortune to one who has never sought such for thee?"

"Doth a man bring ill fortune when he comes in friendship, then, Mistress? I have that which—" He was fumbling with the packet.

"Thou bringest ill fortune by thy very favor, Master Elkins. A man bespoke seeks not other doorsteps—"

He was looking angry, his face flushed, his black brows drawing together in a scowl.

"False! I am not bespoke."

"Tell that then to Master Dimsdale, who hath said that his Patience makes ready her household linens."

"What my father may have promised in my name will not bind me!" he exploded.

"Thou knowest well the law. An undutiful son may well walk in fear of a rope about his throat. I care not what trouble thou makest for thyself—"

"Thou wags a sour tongue, Mistress. The cause of that be plain. None seekest thee out for wooing, thus thou wouldst have it—"

"I would have it that none do speak either of witchcraft about me and mine," she interrupted him sharply. "If thou dost hold favor, thou will not bring danger in thy train."

"Witchcraft!" He took a step backward.

"Aye and aye! A wise woman hath always that to find fearsome. There are those ready to rise up and say thou art beguiled. Think on that, Seth Elkins! Think well on that!"

He still scowled, and threw the packet from him to fall near her skirts.

"Tittle-tattle of clacking women!"

"Have it as thou wilt, it can well be so. Leave this house in peace—"

"Seth!"

At the sound of his name the man turned swifty. Another woman had come near, not from the direction of the herb garden but around the house. She stood looking from Tamar to Seth and back again, and she was smiling. But Holly felt a little shiver down her back; that was not the kind of smile she would ever want to face.

The newcomer was dressed much as Tamar, except her skirts were of what looked to be a finer material, her apron was pure white, and her cap had a narrow edge of lace for a border, as did the collar about her shoulders. Her face was narrow with a tight disapproving mouth and a long sharp nose, while her hair, which was strained back under her cap, was of a sandy red. Her lashes and brows were so pale they looked almost as if she had none at all, and her eyes were small and mean looking. Holly hated her on sight.

"Good morrow, Goody," she said to Tamar. "I see thou art busied, and it be meet I return at a better time."

"There be no time better than this, Mistress Patience." Tamar looked and sounded calm enough. "It be rather Master Elkins who must be about his affairs."

"His affairs?" echoed Patience. "It would seem that his affairs are many. And some of them unknown." She laughed drily.

"Aaaugh!" The sound Seth Elkins made was one of anger. He wheeled about, strode back through the herb garden as if he wished he could use his hands, which were now balled into fists, against the whole world.

Watching him go, Patience spoke. "Thou playest dangerous games, Goody."

"I play no games, Mistress. I do not summon all who come to this door. That be well known—"

"Be it? There be many stories we have heard of dealings with the powers of the dark, Goody, and what can aid a woman who wishes a man enough to invoke them—"

"Aye, there be tales enough, Mistress," Tamar replied, as the other paused. "But such are many times idle chatter. All know I deal only in the healing of men and animals, not to their harming. As has been proven here many times over."

"True." Patience nodded. But there was that in her expression which was threatening, Holly was sure. "And here be I keeping thee from those innocent labors, Goody. Thee has ready the mint? My father hath taken a mighty liking for it, saying hath powers to cure his distress of stomach after a full u....g."

"I have it." Tamar turned to come back inside and then she hesitated. Holly could see she was uneasy. Was it because they were there?

Holly looked back at the table, from which Crock and Judy were watching her. She made gestures with her hands, suggesting they take to cover. Judy looked bewildered. But Crock jerked his head in agreement and caught at his twin, urging her toward the far end of the room, where there was a bed built against the wall. He pushed Judy ahead of him to crawl under the bed. And Holly was following when she brushed against the edge of the table and sent one of the sticky plates clattering to the floor.

She had meant to snatch up the jacket Judy had left behind, but now she had no time, only headed wildly for the bed and crawled under it, jamming against Crock.

"Stupid!" he hissed in her ear.

"And who else finds his way here this morning, Goody?" Patience's voice reached them clearly.

"No one."

"No one, thou sayest? Does no one wear such a jerkin as this, then? Green it be. Aye, and know we not what manner of strange folk weareth green? Many a tale of those we have heard."

"Overseas, mayhap, but here—they come not," Tamar returned.

"Then who hath left a green jerkin? One made of strange cloth. For this I swear be of no honest spin or weave. Look upon it, Goody—that thou must swear to also. Nor is it made for any mortal men, being too small for the wearing by such. This I will take to show—"

"You will not!" Before either Crock or Holly could grab her, Judy hurled herself from under the bed, skimming on her stomach before she could rise to her feet. Then she ran forward. Holly squirmed out after her. Judy was already tugging fiercely at the jacket Patience held. "You give me that! It's mine, Mom bought it for me—"

"Judy!" Holly cried out in despair.

Patience backed against the wall, staring at Judy as if she were some sort of wild animal. She gave a short cry as Holly joined her sister, and released the jacket, which Judy hugged to herself, scowling fiercely at Patience over it.

"You thief!" she accused shrilly.

"Imps—imps of Satan!" Patience continued along the wall with a sidewise movement. "I—let me be! I be christened Christian. Thou cannot come nigh—"

Still facing them, she reached the door, to back through it.

"I'm not either!" Judy looked frightened and ready to cry. "I'm no imp of Satan!"

Holly put her arm about her sister. "Of course you're not. She's just a silly old fusser. We—I think we'd better get out of here."

Crock came to them. "That one's trouble, real trouble," he said. "What are you going to do?" he asked Tamar now.

"We—have we made a lot of trouble for you?" Holly asked in turn. "If we get away fast, you can say she was making up a story about seeing us, can't you?"

Now that it had happened, there was no sign of uneasiness or trouble in Tamar's face.

"I will do what must be done, done well," she said. There was a confident note in her voice, as if she were certain of that. But Holly still felt unhappy and unconvinced.

"We'd better get going," Crock urged. "If that Patience goes and gets someone else—we don't belong here and they'll know it right away."

"Aye, it is best that thou goest," Tamar agreed. "But not without that which thou came for."

She had gone purposefully back to the shelves in the cupboard behind her.

"We didn't come for anything, really," Holly protested. "Just because Judy had this dream and said she had to, and we followed her—"

"Ah, but dreams have uses, my little maid. Thee came because it was meant. These thou wilt take with thee, plant and tend, plant and tend as thy granny will tell thee." She had been filling a small bag of coarse material with some small packets, several bundles of what looked to be dried roots. "It be coiled time which brought thee, coiled time may now release all it binds. Weary waiting—" For a moment she looked so tired and unhappy. Then that shadow was gone from her face, and she was again brisk and pleasant-seeming. "Even time hath an end. Tomkit, rouse thee, it be back again for thee also."

Tomkit leaped lightly from the chair where he had been resting, stretched his legs both fore and aft, and trotted to the door. Tamar stood smiling.

"Will we see you again?" Judy resisted Holly's attempt to hurry her along.

"That be as will be. All things hath a season. Merry meet, merry part, and blessed be."

She raised her hand now and gestured in the air between them. Holly could see that it was not a good-bye wave but must have some other meaning. Then they went out, following Tomkit. At the edge of the maze, without a word among themselves, they turned once to look back. All looked so peaceful under the sun. There was no sign of Tamar. But Holly felt a foreboding. What had they done in allowing Patience to see them—and—and—?

Crock pulled her arm. "Come on. Better get going before anyone else comes along."

As the green walls of the maze closed about them, Holly tried to put in order both her thoughts and her fears.

"We—we aren't in the same world—" she ventured.

"Not in the same *time*," Crock corrected her. "There was a guy that came to science assembly back home last year. He talked about time—and how some people really believe you can fall through time—"

"We—we can get back?" Judy demanded, her voice suddenly shrill with fear. "We *can* get back to the barn-house—to Mom, Grandpa, and Grandma?"

She began to run. They had to race along after her, ahead of the gray shade of Tomkit sliding easily. In and out, back and forth, the way back seemed almost more tangled than it had when they had entered.

Holly had a stitch in her side, and she could hear Judy crying now as she led the way. Then she was calling out, "Mom! Mom!" in gasps of terror, which her older sister would have echoed had she believed that summons would do any good.

The green of the walls about them began to lose its coloring. They were gasping so, they had to cut their run to a stumbling walk. Also it was getting colder. Holly pulled on her jacket, made Judy pause long enough to do likewise. Now all signs of leaves were gone as they burst out into the wasteland and caught sight of the barn roof in the distance.

It was only when she saw the barn-house that Holly was free of her great fear. They *had* gotten back. She turned to look behind her. There were no tall cats and old gate now. Just a thick mass of underbrush, which she did not believe even one as small and agile as Tomkit could wriggle a way through.

"It's—it's like it never happened," she said.

"And we keep it that way," Crock declared. "You hear, Judy, Holly, we keep our mouths shut about this. Nobody would believe us and—"

"But we have this." Holly pointed to the bag Judy held. "The things to plant."

"Pitch 'em back!" Crock ordered.

"*No!*" Judy came to life. "Tamar said to plant them.

We're going to—we can do that much, I think." Holding the bag close, she pushed ahead.

Holly looked at Crock and shrugged. They both knew that Judy was not to be argued with now. Better do some thinking about how they were going to explain the bag and its contents when they got home—a good explanation without telling the whole, unbelievable truth.

5 First Planting

Holly looked to Crock. "What do we tell Grandma—if Judy gives her all that stuff?"

He kicked at a clod of half frozen mud. "I don't know."

"And Tamar—what's going to happen to her? That

Seth Elkins, he talked as if he were mad with her, too."
Quickly Holly explained what she had seen and heard at
the window. "And Tamar, she might be called a witch.
With that Patience seeing us—"

Crock looked at her curiously. "It was in another time,
you know. Whatever happened there must have happened
a long time ago." Only he looked uneasy, as if that
thought gave him little comfort. Tamar was too real. She
could not just be a dream, or someone long ago—

"Remember what Mrs. Pigot said." Holly pulled together her thoughts. "She said Dimsdale had been cursed
by a witch, a long time ago. But Tamar—"

Somehow her thoughts would not fit there. Holly *knew*
there was no ill will in Tamar.

"She couldn't have been a witch, one who cursed people! Though that Patience, she was a Dimsdale—"

"How do you know that?" Crock demanded.

Again Holly pointed out that what she had overheard
proved it.

"So this Seth Elkins, he was supposed to be engaged to
Patience Dimsdale, only he came to see Tamar, brought
her a present," said Crock slowly.

Holly shook her head. "I don't think it was like that,
not really. He seemed mad at Tamar, too. As if she were
stopping him from doing something, as if it weren't really
Tamar he came to see."

"But she was the only one there," Crock pointed out.
"And she didn't talk about anyone else living with her."

"Yes. Only—only it didn't seem as if he liked Tamar
very well. Oh, I'm all mixed up! Crock, do you suppose
we'll ever know what happened? I don't want anything
bad to happen to Tamar—"

"If it did really happen," Crock said, "and it was in

olden days, then maybe it ought to be in a book or something. Your class goes to the library Monday, don't they? Why don't you try to find out there? 'Member what Grandma said about Miss Noyes always being after old books?"

Crock made good sense, though sometimes Holly hated to admit it. Now she demanded to know if he had any ideas about how they were going to keep Judy quiet.

"Don't you try to tell her," he returned. "When you tell people what to do, Holly, you only make them *not* want to do it the harder. Let me see—"

He spurted ahead to catch up with Judy. Holly turned for a last look back at the tangled wilderness where the maze had been. The place bore no likeness now to the green gate, with its cat guardians of the pleasant ways beyond which led to Tamar's place. Was it always summer there? Holly wondered. Could a person be caught in one time and held as if she were shut into a room and the key turned in the lock? And, if that were true, why could Tamar not have gotten out as they got in? What had the pillow to do with it all?

The loud clang of a bell startled her so much she gave a little jump. Grandma's house bell! Which meant it was dinner time! She had warned them about that the first day they had come. Holly, her back to the mysterious mass of entwined bushes, trotted toward the barn-house.

She caught up with Crock just inside the door as he had shucked his windbreaker, heading for the wash basins. Judy was not in sight and Grandma was busy at the stove, her back conveniently turned in their direction.

"Judy?" Holly shaped the name rather than said it.

Crock nodded vigorously which Holly could only accept to mean that he had persuaded his twin not to talk about their morning's activities, at least not yet. But he could not stop her sudden question at the table.

"Grandma, when it's winter—how do you keep your herb plants alive?"

Holly wished she were close enough to deliver a warning kick, but Crock was between them. She glowered at her sister. Judy either could or would not see her.

"Well now—most o' 'em, they jus' take care o' themselves in th' patch. Some—they's more delicate an' they can't take frost. Them I brings into th' big shed where Luther does his workin' with wood. There's a fire there t'other end an' that keeps th' freeze out. Set me up a little garden there, I have. You take a look-see when you is done eatin'."

Judy, spooning up one of Grandma's stews, thanked her through an overfull mouth. Holly sighed with relief: Crock had made his warning, sure enough. Judy could put her bag back in there somewhere, and perhaps Grandma would not notice it at all. Then, in the spring, they could plant what Tamar had given them. Holly relaxed, and for the first time really enjoyed her food.

"Grandpa"—before Holly was aware of the danger Crock spoke now—"those Dimsdales, the ones who owned this place once, they were here an awfully long time, weren't they?"

"Before they even took to lay out Sussex town, far's I heard it." Grandpa was transferring a generous spoonful of jam onto a round of bread. "You better ask your Grandma. She used t' listen to all old Miss Elvery's tales. Lived in th' past, old Miss Elvery did, more'n in th' rightful times. I 'member how once she came down to this here barn all dressed up an' wanted as how I should take out th' carriage an' drive her into some party or other in town. Lawsy, that there carriage had been broken up for years, an' the two horses—they was dead an' gone. People she talked about—they was a-lyin' out in the churchyard, too. But she was certain sure they was just a-waitin' for her to come to see 'em. Took your grandma th' better part of an hour to talk her back to th' house. But you couldn't ever talk her back into th' right time. She wouldn't have a clock runnin' in her whole house. Said as how those there made the time pass, an' if one didn't be lookin' at 'em all day long one could just get on top of time, not be burdened down with it."

He bit off a generous amount of the thickly spread bread and then nodded. "Don't know but what she had a point right there. Time is queer-like. When you do somethin' as you want, it speeds along jus' like one of them big 'planes which can go 'round th' world in a day or so. But if you have to put up with some measlin' little job as makes you want to throw somethin' right across th' room, then that just lasts forever."

Holly had stopped eating and was listening closely. She had never really thought about time before. Oh, she had heard a lot about it—such as "too late to do this," "we'll be early," "hurry now, there's not much time." Over and over again people said things just like that. But what Grandpa said was true. If you liked doing something, then time went so fast you were provoked; and if you were unhappy or bored, time dragged and dragged.

"But you asked did the Dimsdales be here long—yes, they were. Mercy, didn't Grandma tell you a whole book-like of stories 'bout them an' all their hard luck an' all?"

"Why were they so unlucky?" Holly asked then.

"Now that be a question." Grandma pushed back in her

chair as if she were going to make another flying trip to the stove for second helpings all around, but she did not get up. "Miss Elvery—a kinder lady never set foot on this earth! She would do her best for any poor soul as was in need. But it seems like every time she tried to help herself—well, it turned out th' worse for her. Th' last time, when that slick crook got her railroad shares offen her, she was really broke down. Said as how it was th' witch's curse, an' noways could it go from Dimsdale or them what had Dimsdale blood in 'em. But she was beginnin' to fail then, poor old lady—an' she thought too much 'bout all the misfortunes as she had had to face."

"What was the curse?" Holly thought that Grandma was not going to answer, that she was even displeased by this bald question.

"That's foolish talk, child. People in town, when they don't know it all, they make up stuff to say. An' Miss Elvery, she was so borne down by all her troubles, she was like to believe that th' Good Lord had truly turned His face from her. But it was foolishment for sure. Best you hear it right—'cause if they still talk about it in town you may hear it like it never was.

"Miss Elvery showed me once a old book, she could hardly read in it. All hand-wrote it was, with queer old writing—faded so you had to take one o' them magnifyin' glasses to see it at all. It was a kind of journal as was kept by a man who lived here. He put down all kinds of things—like what he paid for stuff he bought, how he sowed his fields, th' harvests he had. An' in between, other bits, 'bout his family and himself. Who was born an' who died an' the like.

"He was a kinda hard old man—his name was Sexton Dimsdale—mighty hard on them as lived under him. In those days the master of the house, well—he could just about do as he pleased an' nobody dared cross him, 'specially no woman. 'Cause in those days, women, they weren't o' much account, 'cept to keep house an' feed an' clothe an' do 'bout all the work as kept that house running. Men like this Sexton Dimsdale, he never took 'count of how comfortable his womenfolk did make him.

"This Sexton, he had a cravin' for land, more'n more of it. He built a bigger house—this here barn, to this side with the fireplace an' all, was his first house. But that was far too small to suit him. No sirree, he wanted a big house so everybody in Sussex would be 'mazed to see. He brought a man clean over from England to plan his big house, an' lay out his garden. Not that he had a likin' for growin' things—but because he wanted it all for show.

"An' this man, he had women kin he brought along. He had a 'greement with Mr. Dimsdale that he was to have land for hisself in part payment for what he did. It was all clear in writin' an' legal. But he died 'afore he quite finished th' garden part. Then Mr. Dimsdale, he tried by law to get back the part he had given this man. But the Judge, he stood up to Mr. Dimsdale. He was a Pigot, an' they never took to be good friends. So then Mr. Dimsdale had to leave that part of th' land as it was —with the little house th' plannin' man built on it and his family a-still living there. He had one daughter as was a great gardener—she was one with th' healin' gift, too, knew all about herbs an' such.

"There weren't many doctors then, an' those who were, didn't know too much. People in Sussex, they would go to this healin' woman for help 'fore they called in th' doctor. She didn't push herself in much but lived quiet, an' people liked her.

"But every time Mr. Dimsdale thought about her livin' on what he believed was rightfully his land, he'd get madder. He had a daughter as wasn't much to look at. But his sons, they died of a fever, so she was all he had left. So he looked around to get her a husband as would be a credit to the Dimsdales. 'Cause he was so puffed up about his family now he acted like they were lords, like in th' old country.

"Th' Elkins—they was th' other comin' family in Sussex. Near as land-rich and merchants besides, trading with th' Indians and doin' very well with it. There was an Elkins son—an' him old Sexton picked upon for his daughter. Things was run a lot different in them old days. Even if a son or daughter was all grown up, maybe even had themselves families o' their own, leastwise were old enough to have 'em, still they had to do as their father told 'em. Miss Noyes, she showed me a queer old book o' laws once, an' it said right there, for a judge to see, that did a boy be disobedient to what his folks wanted—he could be hung! Think o' that now!

"Well, th' Elkins son, he didn't take kindly to th' idea o' weddin' old Sexton's daughter, but he didn't have much say in it, 'cause his father promised for him. But he took to visitin' the healin' woman on th' sly, an' Dimsdale found out.

"In those days it was easy to call witch 'gainst a woman who knew herbs an' such an' who kept to herself a lot. An' the healin' woman, she didn't have no one to speak up for her."

Grandma paused. Holly leaned forward.

"What happened, Grandma?"

"Now that is where the part of the book Miss Elvery had gets confusin'. Halloween—that was a witches' night an' people feared them th' worst at that time. So Dimsdale, he got together his men an' they made a plan to grab th' witch (as he called her) on Halloween, just when she was busy at her witching—an' maybe burn her an' her house all up together."

"No!" Judy's voice was a loud cry, startling them all.

Grandma looked distressed. "There—I did get carried 'way tellin' all that, an' I should've forgot it long ago. T'aint a good story for tellin' at any time."

"Grandma, they didn't burn the witch—they didn't!" Judy protested.

"Well, no, they didn't. It's a very queer story all around. They went to do it, yes. Then somethin' strange happened. Some real live devilish things came out of nowhere—an' all the men ran. When they got up courage enough to go back the next day—well, they just couldn't find anything at all; house an' witch were gone. Only th' witch, she had put a curse on old Sexton Dimsdale 'fore the devils saved her. An' she set it to eat at him an' his family as long as they lived. Little by little, she told 'em, it was goin' to eat up all he treasured most until all his fields would be waste an' no one would take comfort from them."

"And it happened that way?" Crock wanted to know.

"Yes, it seems like it did. The Dimsdales didn't have their bad luck all at once, it came little by little, but it did come. Only that's all jus' an old story. Miss Elvery, she was minded to give the book what it was wrote down in to Reverend Burns. She said it was a workin' out o' God's will as could be plainly seen, that the hatred old

Sexton sowed, an' all his greediness, had ripened over the years an' had come to full harvest. But she never did. An' the book was burned up in the fire. Miss Elvery, she tried to repay a lot with her kindness to others.

"When she was dyin' she told me somethin' as I'll never forget—that as how when somethin' is destroyed, it can be rebuilt. But that takes a long time. An' that if Dimsdale —the Dimsdale place, that is—could have in return what had gone from it, all would be well. Poor lady, she tried to do some of that her ownself."

"But they did not get the witch?" Judy persisted.

"Not if that old book has it set down right. Only where could a house an' a woman jus' vanish to? That's the least likely part of the whole story. Seems like old Sexton, he might have had somethin' to hide—I don't know. Speakin' of time, look yonder! This is no day to be dawdling! Your mom will be in on the two o'clock bus, an' Luther, you'd best take off right now to pick her up."

"I got all them things for Mr. Correy," Grandpa said, and he looked a little unhappy. "Won't be much room in the truck—"

Holly knew what he meant: no room for them. For a moment she was going to protest, to demand that there be room. Then she saw Grandma glance in her direction, and she knew that she could not be so babyish.

"Judy can squeeze in maybe," she suggested, though she hated to say it. "And Crock can ride in the back—"

"No." Judy, to Holly's entire surprise, answered positively. "Mom'll be tired. If I ride in the truck, I'll have to sit on her lap. And I don't want her to have me bump-bumping on her all the way here. We'll stay."

Grandma gave a quick smile. "Good enough. An' you can lend a helpin' hand right here. This mornin', I got

a real good start made on my statue. Was you to do th'
dishes now—an' th' like—I could set my mind to ease
at gettin' on with that."

So Holly found herself washing dishes with a care
she might not have used at home, intent on doing the
task so well that Grandma could see a difference. Meanwhile, Grandma put out her broken lady on the table
and gave her glasses such an emphatic thump up into
place on her nose that Holly believed they would not dare
to slide down again, at least for a good long while.

She would have liked to watch Grandma working, but
that might be a bother. It sometimes was when one con-
centrated on a hard job. And, as Judy hung up the last
dishtowel, she jerked her head toward the door.

"We're going out, Grandma," Holly said.

"All right. Don't go wandering off—"

Tomkit arose from the piece of rag carpet in front of
the wide hearthstone to come with them. As they passed
out the door, Holly saw that Judy had the bag Tamar
had given to her pressed tightly against her under her
arm.

"Grandma said in the fix-it shed," she said as she
went. "That's over here."

The fix-it shed was really a part of the barn, added on
later, but with no door into the barn at all, only one outside. It smelled of glue, paint, and oil, and the whole of
one end was a workbench with rows of tools hung up
neatly on the wall over it. There was a half partition
made of three old doors fitted together into a wall.
Beyond that was Grandma's wintertime garden. On
the floor, on shelves, crowding most of a table, which
was another door set on legs, were pots with things

growing in them. Small bags, tightly closed, hung on cords all along the walls above the shelves.

Judy dropped on her knees to peer into the darkened cave which existed under the table.

"Pots here, lots of them, and nothing in them," she announced, and began to pull out those she could reach.

Holly remembered how Mom had planted her African violets when they had to be repotted.

"We don't have any planting soil like Mom gets," she objected.

Judy squatted back on her heels. "These are supposed to grow in regular dirt—Dimsdale dirt. We just dig enough to fill the pots. You take that little trowel and that old basket over there."

There was something about Judy's calm certainty that this was what must be done which led Holly to take up the trowel and the basket. Surely there was more to planting than just digging up some common old dirt, putting it in pots, and then pushing seeds or roots in to hope those would grow. Only neither she nor Judy knew what that might be.

She did look around outside before she dug. There seemed to be flower beds along the other wall of the barn. And it was there she went to work, taking dirt, not all from one place so a hole would be noticed, but a trowelful here and one there. Three times she filled the basket and lugged it back to Judy, who used the stiff clumps of soil to fill the pots.

As Holly worked she thought about Grandma's story— of how the Dimsdales had tried to destroy both Tamar and her house. That Tamar was the woman Sexton Dimsdale had called the witch, Holly had no doubt.

Only she found it hard to believe that Tamar was really a witch—or that her curse had lain so heavy on the Dimsdales. Witches were a part of fairy stories as far as Holly was concerned.

Of course, their own adventure today—that was not a part of real life, either. Had Tamar and her house gone into some strange turn of time and been there just as they were for all these years and years? But why, then, would Seth Elkins and Patience Dimsdale have been there, too? They were enemies, and Tamar would not have willingly taken them with her.

Suppose—suppose where they had been today was a time *before* Sexton Dimsdale had done his best to get at the witch. Then, if they could return, warn Tamar— Yes! Holly, stooping a little under the weight of a basket of dark soil, stopped short before the door of the fix-it shed. If they could warn Tamar of what was coming— they must warn her!

In the morning they could try the maze again. No, they could not, either. Mom would be here. Holly pushed open the shed door. They would have to wait, maybe until next week. And the pillow. Judy had slept on the pillow and then had known just how to get into the maze. Maybe that was a necessary part of finding Tamar again. If it was, then this time Holly would sleep on it.

She was determined about that. After all, she was the oldest, she knew what they must do to help Tamar. It was—it was even her duty to see that they got back to Tamar's house and helped her.

But Holly said nothing of her plan as she helped Judy plant seeds and roots, brought water in a pail to sprinkle over the lumpy earth.

"Where are you going to put them?" she asked at last,

surveying the row of pots. "Grandma's surely going to see them and ask questions if you leave them out here."

"I know. I've been thinking about that. So we put them in back along the shelves, in and out so the ones Grandma has already there will be all around them. Like this." Judy picked up the nearest pot, moved two with a luxuriant green growth on one shelf, slipped hers in behind, and used the two others as a screen.

"That's neat!" Holly agreed, and went to work in the same fashion.

When they had finished, the pots were certainly so well mixed in with Grandma's that you would not have known they had been added unless you were told—or so Holly hoped.

She and Judy swept up the spilled dirt, wiped off the trowel, and returned the basket to its place. The green fresh smell in here reminded Holly of the maze with the sunlit garden beyond.

She was trying to recall all the details of that when Judy spoke: "Where do you suppose Tamar and the house went, Holly, when those bad men came to hurt her? Was—was she really a witch who could fly off and take her house with her?"

"That's only a fairy tale, Judy—you're getting old for them. I don't know where Tamar went."

"Maybe she hid in time."

Holly was startled. "What do you mean?"

"It's something like Grandpa was saying about how time is so different. When I have a toothache, like I did last winter when we couldn't get Dr. Williams for two whole days, then it seemed the pain just went on for ever and ever. And that last day Daddy was with us when we went to the zoo and had dinner—that day went so fast it never seemed to be real after, more like I dreamed it. I always thought time meant clocks, seeing the hands go around to tell you to do this or that before it was too late. But now I wonder what time really is. Maybe you could pick out some happy day, if you knew just how to do it, and just stay in that day for always and always—"

Judy gazed at Holly as if she wanted to be reassured that this idea, fantastic as a fairy tale, might indeed come true.

When Holly did not answer, Judy continued: "Men fly up and walk on the moon, while we can sit here right in our own houses and watch them do it. I'll bet in the old days people would have thought that was real magic or a fairy story and could never come true. But maybe in the olden days people like Tamar had their way of knowing about other things—like hiding in time. I want to be sure Tamar is safe, Holly, I want to!"

"So do I. Maybe we can, later," Holly was beginning, when they heard a loud honk of a horn.

"Mom!" Judy slammed out of the door, ran toward the drive on the other side of the barn-house. And Holly, all her ideas about another trip into the maze forgotten for the moment, sped after her.

Mom came out of the cab of the truck as if she could hardly wait for it to come to a stop, and opened her arms wide so somehow Judy and Holly reached her together and were tangled up in one big hug. Mom was back—that was all that mattered now, and all else was forgotten. This slice of time they must make last as long as possible.

6 Witches and Curses

Now it happened, as Grandpa had pointed out, that this good time went so fast it was over before the Wades really enjoyed it. When they saw Mom back on the bus late Sunday afternoon, it seemed she had hardly had a chance to say hello before she was saying good-bye again, waving through the window as the bus drew away from them.

Ahead was not one long week but four before she would be here again, because she had promised to take extra duty so she could get off three days at Thanksgiving. And Thanksgiving seemed so distant now that it might well be a whole year away.

When the girls were back in their room, Holly remembered one thing—the pillow. But they could not— *she* could not—try sleeping on that tonight, not with tomorrow a school day. However, she could make sure it was safe for when she might use it.

"What did you do with the pillow, Judy?"

Judy was rubbing Tomkit under the chin in a way he particularly enjoyed. His eyes were nearly closed as he purred loudly. She did not even look up as she answered, "It's in the box, my box of cloth pieces, in the wardrobe."

Holly wanted to make sure of that. With Mom gone, she was thinking about Tamar, about how they had to get back and warn her. She sighed; there was no use trying —not until Friday night. And, like Thanksgiving, that seemed a very long time away.

Monday this week was special. Holly's class was scheduled to go to the library. Mrs. Finch had announced "special projects." In spite of her carefully preserved determination not to be noticed, Holly discovered that "special projects" might be exciting. Sussex was going to have a birthday in the coming spring, a three-hundred-year-old birthday. Now "special projects" meant that one chose a subject concerning the town history, to make a booklet from what facts one found out. Or else one could make something with one's hands to show what the people who had founded Sussex had had in their homes, or worn, or known.

Today's visit to the library was to start the special-project program because the library itself was in a very old house, one of the oldest still standing in the town. There was a museum there, too, full of things from the earlier days.

"You all can see what references are available," Mrs. Finch said. "Then, after we return you will make your choice of subject, handing it in on a written slip with your name and grade."

Holly looked carefully at the library as they came along the leaf-strewn walk toward it. It was a lot larger than Tamar's house, but the chimney was also in the middle, and the windows were as high in the walls. Only these walls were of brick, and the roof was covered with slates, not mossy green shingles.

Mrs. Finch lined up the children before they went in and pointed out the brick, which had been made in a clay pit once down by the river. Then she explained to them about the windows. "They once were all small diamond-shaped panes set in lead," she said.

Unconsciously Holly nodded, comparing what she saw now with Tamar's house.

"But during the Revolution," Mrs. Finch continued, "that lead was used to make bullets. So for a while people went back to using windows of oiled deerhide shaved thin. After the war these larger pieces of glass were brought in.

"Now, remember this is a library," she continued as they started in. "You will conduct yourselves with the proper attention—"

Mrs. Finch always spoke that way, with a sharp now-come-to-order note in her voice. And somehow it worked. She was a no-nonsense person and everyone knew it.

To Holly, used to the large city libraries, this was a very small, cramped space. There were only two rooms, the fireplace serving each. Books were packed very tightly together on the shelves. And there was little room left for the benches and chairs which had been brought into the smaller room to seat the class.

On upper shelves and in a little side cubby were other things than books, too. One whole shelf was given to birds' nests—*birds' nests*—each with a white tag on the front. Then there was a picture made of seeds, and some shells, and behind them a row of frames which held what looked to be brownish sheets of paper. There were live plants, too, and a big glass bowl which had tiny growing things in it, as if someone had just scooped up a couple of trowelfuls of a very small country and plunked it down in a giant's fish globe.

Miss Noyes, the librarian, began to talk then, and Holly grew intent. She spoke about their projects and the town birthday. What she said didn't sound like school history, all dates and far-off happenings—this was about people. As she spoke, Miss Noyes held up a sampler and explained how a girl a lot younger even than Judy had made it, and showed a pistol which had been carried by a soldier who went to Valley Forge, and then a string of beads which was real Indian money—wampum—like in the stories about the Pilgrims. Holly had a feeling that she was being drawn in, made a part of all that had once been. History was a long march of people, some of them far off in the distance, others just a little ahead, but people like herself, and Grandpa,

Grandma, Mom—Dad. Suddenly Holly realized history was not just a page in a book, it was people!

Miss Noyes went on to speak of books now. Not the history books one had at school, but books the earlier people had read—and had written!

Again Holly was startled. That old book Miss Noyes was holding up for them all to see, it was written by hand, not printed, and the writing was so old and faint you could hardly see it at all. Was it like the book Grandma had talked about, the one old Miss Elvery had had?

". . . journal of Seth Elkins," Miss Noyes continued.

Seth Elkins! The same Seth who had come to see Tamar? Had he put in that book what had happened to Tamar? Dared Holly ask without telling why she wanted to know? But already Miss Noyes had carefully closed the book and fitted it back in a box, and she was speaking about the museum and how they would see a spinning wheel and a flax loom—

To Holly's disappointment Mrs. Finch beckoned them to follow her, and the class had to file off to the museum. There was plenty there to see, and Holly went slowly. But her mind was only half on what she viewed and on Mrs. Finch's explanations. Rather, she was thinking of Seth Elkins' journal. Had Miss Noyes read it all the way through? Could she tell more about what happened at Dimsdale on that Halloween so very long ago? At that instant Holly knew what she was going to take for her project—Dimsdale itself.

Because of that, if Mrs. Finch agreed, she could ask questions. Maybe even learn what was in the journal, and what had happened to Tamar. Of course, she did not dare tell what she knew now. But she could use bits later, as if she had read them, such as the description of Tamar's house, and the maze, and the herb garden—

She was so lost in her plan that she walked right into a girl a little ahead who had stopped to show a friend a framed sampler hanging on the museum wall.

"See—right there—my name—Rebecca Eames. My grandmother gave that to hang in the museum. 'Cause her great-great—I don't know how many times back now—made it. And—who do you think you're shoving?" Becky Eames whirled about toward Holly. "Just 'cause you come from Boston, you think you know everything! Well, you don't, see. Your great-great-great-grandmother hasn't got a sampler hanging up here, has she?"

Holly stiffened. Here it came at last, what she had been expecting ever since she had stepped aboard the school bus that first day. Now she would be told she lived in a dump, she was black, all the other things she knew she would have said to her, and about her, sooner or later.

Becky's friend (it was Martha Torrey, Holly saw, another one of them) pulled at Becky's sleeve. "Becky! Remember what Mrs. Finch said—"

Holly could guess what *that* was, and it made her even madder inside. She didn't need Mrs. Finch to go around warning people not to say this or that because she was black and lived in a dump.

"And just what did Mrs. Finch say?" she demanded fiercely. "Sure I live in a junkyard with the junk! And I'm black, too! You afraid some of that'll rub off on you? Well, it won't. I may be black but I'm not dirty, see! And you and your old Mrs. Finch can just mind your own business."

She turned away as Martha said quickly, "No, Holly, you've got it all wrong, truly you——"

Scowling, Holly looked back over her shoulder. "I've got it all right. I have had, ever since I came to this stupid old school."

She hurried on, to stand impatiently at the library door, ready to be gone just as soon as Mrs. Finch started them off. Inside, her anger grew. She had been going to take Dimsdale for her project—now she had a better idea. She was going to write about witches, about how that old Sexton Dimsdale had made trouble because he was greedy and ignorant, and how he got what he deserved. That was going to be her project! She hoped now that the legend was true—that Tamar had been a real witch and had cursed Sexton Dimsdale just as Miss Elvery had said. He deserved it! Everyone in this town should have been cursed—

It was noon when they got back to the school. Holly singled out Judy, who seemed reluctant to come. She was talking with that same Debbie who had wanted to share lunches with her before, as Holly bore grimly down upon them. Judy ought to know better; Holly had told her often enough what to expect. Now it looked almost as if Judy were not going to come along, even when Holly beckoned to her to hurry.

"I don't see why," she burst out, "you never want to be friends with anybody. I like Debbie——"

"Be friends!" Holly exploded. "They don't want to be friends! Just like this morning—that Becky Eames was quick enough to say we had no right to be part of Sussex, we don't belong!"

"She said that—right out?" Judy looked troubled. "But —why, Holly?"

"You know why." Holly scowled. Of course, Becky had not said quite that, but it was certainly what she had meant. The sooner Judy realized the truth, the better for her. "We live in a junkyard, and we're black."

"But Jimmie Little, and the Woods girls"— Judy stopped and pointed across the room—"they're black and no one seems to care. Jimmie goes around with Ralph Bingley and Jud Torrey all the time. And Sally and Betsy Woods sing in the junior choir and—look at Crock, he's over there now with Phil Noyes and the Byfield boys, and they like him!"

"He'll find out," Holly said grimly. "And Jimmy and the Woods'—they lived here a long time—maybe people forget. They don't live in a dump, either."

Judy looked mutinous, but she sat down beside Holly with a sigh and opened her lunch box. "You decided," she asked as she unwrapped her topmost sandwich, "what you're going to do for your special project? I have. I told Mrs. Dale, and she thought mine was good enough to write up on the board—the first one."

"What is it?" Holly delayed answering, by asking a question of her own.

"Herb gardens, like Tamar's—"

"Judy, you didn't tell?" Holly demanded.

" 'Course not! But Grandma uses herbs, and lots of people do now—Grandma has some real, real old books about how they used such things even more in the olden days. I'm going to make rose beads, when there're roses, and one of those clove oranges which smell nice, and maybe sugared mint leaves. And I'm going to learn about those you can use as medicine like Tamar did to help people." She was smiling again, her disagreement with Holly forgotten. "I can write about Tamar's garden, even if I don't say where it was—"

Holly was surprised, and inwardly a little uneasy. Judy was so sure of herself now. Back in Boston she had listened to Holly, and she would have asked Holly what she thought before telling Mrs. Dale about her subject project. She was doing a lot of things for herself lately. There was the way she had taken command and found how to plant Tamar's gifts in what Holly acknowledged was a clever manner. Judy had always been the follower where Holly led; now it appeared that she was finding new paths for herself.

"You'd better be careful what you say," Holly said with more emphasis than she really planned.

Judy's smile faded. "There you go again, Holly Wade. Always telling me what to do! I'm getting tired of you—"

Holly's irritation became alarm. Judy, if Judy were going to be stubborn— They had always done things together, things Holly had planned. Judy had seemed content enough to agree. Holly knew there were instances when Judy could not be pushed, but those had been rare and had not lasted long. What if Judy were going to be that way all the time? Quickly Holly tried to make matters better.

"I just was afraid you might say something without thinking."

"The way you talk, you'd believe I wasn't any older than Lissy Jones back home. And she's three whole years younger than me. I don't go blabbing around everything I know, Holly Wade."

"I know," Holly answered. Judy might have to be coaxed back into line again. "It's just that even if we stood up, all of us, and told all about Tamar, no one would believe us."

"I suppose so. But she's real, I know that, Holly. And I'm going to learn some of the things she knows. Mrs. Dale said there're a lot of books about herbs and I'm going to ask Grandma to tell me, too. What are you going to take as your project?"

For a moment Holly hesitated. She was still very sure that she had a good plan—to show up that old Sexton Dimsdale, and make people living right here today understand what it meant to call people names which weren't true. Though Becky hadn't, of course, called any names, Holly could imagine right now the ones she might have used, and those made her madder every time she thought of them.

"What are you going to take? Or is it such a great big secret that—" Judy was beginning to get prickly again.

"I'm going to take witches," Holly said in a rush. "How the people in the old times made trouble for people like Tamar and called them witches, and how the Dimsdales were cursed because they did—"

"You said not to tell about Tamar. And now you're going to!" Judy accused.

"I won't tell about us seeing her, nothing like that. I'm going to look it all up in the old books, and ask around. Miss Noyes, at the library this morning, she showed us a journal which she said had been written by Seth Elkins—"

"That Seth who came to see Tamar?" Judy interrupted, her eyes wide.

"I suppose so. Maybe he tells just what did happen. Not that queer story about Tamar and the house disappearing and all."

"But will Mrs. Finch let you write about witches?"

"I'm not going to tell her that I am going to do witches. I'm going to say I want to write about the people who were at Dimsdale, the man who built the big house that burned down."

"I wish we could find out what happened to Tamar," said Judy slowly.

"I know what we do have to do," Holly replied with her old assertiveness. "We've got to get back there somehow and warn Tamar, let her know what Sexton Dimsdale is going to do on Halloween."

"But that was a long time ago," Judy objected. "He's already done it and you can't change anything now."

"Maybe we can. Look here, Judy, we must have gone back in time to a day that was before Halloween—it was summer, wasn't it? Well, if we can get back to that day, we can tell Tamar to watch out—"

"Oh!" Now Judy was nodding vigorously. "Yes. I'll take the pillow Friday night and we'll go back again and tell her."

I'll take the pillow this time, Holly assured herself. Judy had had her turn. Anyway it was her idea, not Judy's. Yes, if anyone slept with the herb pillow this week it was going to be Holly Wade.

She handed in the description of her project, the history of Dimsdale, and Mrs. Finch noted it down in her project book with a nod of agreement.

"It's a pity Miss Dimsdale's family papers were all destroyed in that unfortunate fire," she commented. "The board of the historical museum had asked her several times to deposit them at the library, but she seemed to have a distaste for letting anyone see them. Yet the Dimsdales were a very important part of Sussex. It was on a tract obtained from King Charles by the Dimsdales that Sussex was laid out, you know. You must consult with Miss Noyes; she will know several excellent references for you to use, Holly.

"I wonder if any of the old garden still exists—it was the first formal and carefully planted garden ever to be laid out here, you know. And there is a legend that there even was a maze!"

"Grandma said it's all grown up so tight no one can get in," Holly answered quickly. Mrs. Finch was showing such an interest in her idea that she began to fear she might be *too* interested. Enough to ask some questions Holly was neither prepared to answer nor wanted asked at all.

Mrs. Finch gazed a little beyond Holly, as if seeing the wild part of Dimsdale rather than the wall of the classroom. "I suppose so. But, Holly, if you can make us see Dimsdale as it once was—then you are adding to our picture of Sussex at its beginning. That will be an excellent project."

She paused for a moment before she asked, in a slightly different tone of voice, "Holly, what do you think of Sussex?" Now she looked straight at Holly herself as if she could see into her mind and sort out Holly's thoughts.

"It's—it's different—from Boston, I mean." Holly tried to find words which would not give away her real feelings about all that had happened to her since the telegram had arrived. It was none of Mrs. Finch's business how she felt anyway, she thought. As if Mrs. Finch would really care!

"I imagine so." Mrs. Finch sounded a little sharp, almost as if Holly were being stupid in class. "You've an interesting project, Holly; it is up to you to show what you can do with it."

As Holly went out to the bus, she wondered just what Mrs. Finch would have said if she had told her the *real* project—the cursing of Dimsdale. She glanced along the line of children waiting for the ride home. Grandma had said that people in town talked about the curse, that they'd hear stories. Suppose she would start asking questions? No, probably the kids here wouldn't know. But old people, like Mrs. Pigot who had talked about it the very first time they had mentioned Dimsdale—she ought to know something. And there ought to be other old people who'd remember things. She would have to be mighty careful asking, though.

"Holly!" Judy's voice right in her ear made her jump. "Holly, didn't you hear me? I asked about the Halloween party. It's going to be dress-up, Debbie said. What do you suppose I can wear?"

Holly was drawn entirely out of her plans for detecting the past. "What party?"

"The big school one. They have it every year and everyone dresses up. From four to seven on Halloween. Debbie said we could ride in with her. So you see, Holly, you're not so always right. Debbie likes me and she'd like you, too, if you'd let her. You know what I'd like to be—I've been thinking it over ever since she told me about it—I'd like to be a cat, like Tomkit, gray with big green eyes and a long tail. That would be fun!"

"If it's in town at night, Grandpa and Grandma won't want us to come in." Holly brought out her most formidable argument quickly.

Judy made an impish face. "That's where you're wrong

again, Holly. Grandma, she comes every year, she rides in with Debbie's mom, and she tells fortunes the old way. She makes special doughnuts, too. So there! Do you suppose Grandma could help me make a cat costume, Holly?"

Grandma going to a school party! Holly was surprised all right, surprised and resentful. Grandma had taken lately to asking if Holly knew that girl or this one, and seeming surprised when Holly said just in school. As if she expected Holly to be the most popular girl in the class or something. She did not want to hurt Grandma's feelings by telling the truth—that they weren't wanted. Because Grandma seemed so sure that they would be. Holly had to dodge a lot of questions lately. There could be no appealing to Grandma to stay home from the party, not if things were the way Judy said that they were.

"A cat costume would be a hard one," she answered Judy, full of dismay. If Grandma insisted that they go, and she went with them and saw—

"Grandma's mighty clever with her hands—that's what Mr. Correy said when he came out yesterday afternoon. And it's true. I bet she can make a real cat costume."

Holly tried to push the thought of the Halloween party out of her mind entirely. She did it by thinking of that other Halloween, when the Dimsdales went witch hunting. This, of course, brought her back to Tamar and the warning. Also, if she were to see Tamar again, maybe ask her some questions, she could learn the truth. Whether Tamar really was a witch and had vanished by magic, after cursing Dimsdale—

A witch—if you were a witch you could have your wishes. And make them come true. Right now she could wish Judy would forget all about the party, Grandma also, so they would not have to go. She could wish—

Judy was very full of her project that evening at the supper table, and Grandma got so excited that she had to shove back her glasses every moment or so; they really slipped up and down her nose without coming to a full stop very often. Crock announced his project—what kind of furniture they had had in the first Sussex houses. He had taken lately to going out in the fix-it shed and watching Grandpa, and was very full of information (which did not interest Holly in the least) as to how to mend this and repair that.

She sat very silent herself. Let Judy and Crock do all the talking tonight. Holly wanted to be sure of the questions she was going to ask, beginning with Grandma and Grandpa and what they could remember about Dimsdale before it became a dump, and about Miss Elvery and her stories. It might be well to write those questions all down before she asked them. Then she would be sure they were the right ones and not give away her plan.

When Judy was safely in bed that night, and Holly was certain that she was asleep by the sound of her breathing, she slipped from between the covers and padded over to the wardrobe. Inch by inch she eased the door open until she could feel inside for the lid of Judy's box of cloth pieces. She slipped that off and prodded, until her fingers met the pillow. More than anything in the world she wanted to take it out, to sleep on it tonight, and see if she could get back some way to the house in the maze and Tamar.

But there was no use in trying it. School tomorrow, and the next day, and the next—the next—

Only it did not quite work out that way. For there was a special teachers' meeting on Friday and school would be out at noon. As soon as she heard that, Holly cornered Crock and Judy.

"Friday afternoon," she said eagerly. "We can get back in the maze Friday afternoon, don't you see?"

Crock agreed readily. "All right, better'n Saturday really. Jim's coming by to give us a hand out in the yard then. He wants to hunt up something to fix his bike, if he can find it."

There was no use in reminding Crock of the danger of getting too friendly, Holly had known that from the first. Anyway, if he wanted to get into a fight—and fight he would, if he were called some of the things she could so well imagine—then that was his own fault.

Again time was something she fought all the way to Thursday night. She had discovered before then that neither Judy nor Crock had any idea of allowing her to take the pillow by will alone. No, it would be choosing again. And Holly was determined this time that she would do as she had never done before, make sure she would come out the winner. She *had* to be the one, she *had* to!

Crock held the papers to pull once more, and, in her hand, Holly deliberately bent the one she had drawn. The others were too intent upon their own drawing to see her. If hers was not the shortest paper in the beginning, it would be when she got through with it. And, through her crumpling, it was, over Crock's. Triumphantly, she gathered the pillow to her.

As she settled in bed she thumped her head against it. There was a funny smell, not as good as it had been before. This made her nose itch to sneeze. If she had not been sure, somehow, that this was the only way to get into the maze, she would have shoved the pillow away again. But in spite of the unpleasant smell, which grew stronger, Holly was firm—she *would* dream the way in!

7 Widdershins Way

In the morning she could not remember her dreams,
except that she did know a way into the maze. The rest
—when she tried to recall anything it made her head
ache. Tamar—had she seen Tamar? Holly had an odd

half-remembrance of someone else, quite unlike Tamar. Someone who had smiled and beckoned and whom she must see again. But of course that person must have been Tamar, and she, Holly, would be the one to warn her about the trouble to come.

"You dreamed." Judy was putting on her shoes. "But those must have been bad dreams, Holly."

"Why?" Holly rounded on her defensively.

" 'Cause you called for Mom and said you wanted out—" Judy sat on the edge of the bed, watching her sister closely now. "You talked as if you were shut up somewhere."

Holly tossed her head. "I don't remember. But I do know the way into the maze anyhow. And we'll go this afternoon and see Tamar. You want to do that, don't you?"

To her surprise Judy did not answer at once. "I don't know. I'm going to wait and see—"

"Wait and see about what?" Holly exploded. "The last time you were all ready to go, you wanted us to hurry up. Just 'cause I had the dream this time, now you talk about going to wait and see! What's the matter with you, Judy Wade?"

Judy still measured her sister with that unblinking stare; Holly stirred uncomfortably under it. It was almost as if Judy already knew that Holly had—well, arranged things last night. But Holly had *had* to. Crock did not really care, and they—*she*—had to warn Tamar about all the trouble coming.

"Nothing's the matter, I guess," Judy said slowly. "Only, I guess I didn't like your bad dream."

"But you don't really know it was a bad dream," countered Holly swiftly.

"I know you were crying for Mom to come and get you. And that Tomkit—he got up once and sniffed at the pillow; then he jumped back and hissed and spat, just like he hated it.

"But—oh, well." Judy shrugged. "I guess it's all right."

Of course it was all right, Holly assured herself fiercely not only through breakfast but through the morning at school. When they piled back on the bus after the half-day session, she was only eager to get back to Dimsdale, gobble down lunch, and start into the maze. It was a dark day and the clouds looked heavy, but so far there had been no rain. She kept her fingers crossed all the way home and hoped the storm would hold off.

Holly was so intent upon her worry that she did not listen much to what was going on around her, until she heard Judy say in a voice which carried over the rumble of the bus, "Grandma thinks she can make a cat suit for me. She has a big woolly gray blanket, just as gray as Tomkit."

"Black cats are for Halloween." That was Sandra Hawkins.

"Maybe—but I want to be a gray one," Judy returned. "Tomkit is a special cat, it's more fun to look like him. What are you going to be?"

Sandra giggled. "I don't know, not yet. Usually I wear what Mary wore last year, and she gets a new one. She was a ballet dancer last year. But I got out her costume yesterday and tried it on. It doesn't fit me at all. So I showed Mom and she said she'll see—"

What did Halloween costumes matter now, thought Holly impatiently. If they did have to go to that old party, and it looked as if they would, with Grandma being a part of it, she'd just get together something. Maybe go as a gypsy. That was easy enough: a skirt of one color, and a blouse of another, hoop earrings, and a scarf around her head. But there'd be plenty of time to think about that. What was important was what was going to happen this afternoon.

Today luck was with them. Because Grandma was going off to her sewing circle right after lunch. She made them promise not to go far from the house (the maze was not all that far, Holly assured herself) and to be careful. Grandpa was working in the fix-it shed, and Crock seemed more interested in what he was doing there than in the maze, until Holly reminded him that he had promised to go back with her and Judy.

By the time Grandma at last drove off with Mrs. Wilson, Holly was fairly ready to dance up and down with impatience, which neither Judy nor Crock seemed to share. When she turned on them as the car went down the lane, they were looking, not at her, but doubtfully at each other. As for Tomkit, he had completely disappeared, as if this new expedition were no affair of his whatsoever.

"We had better get going," Holly said.

"I promised Grandpa——" Crock began; then, encountering her fierce glare, he shrugged. "All right. Let's go and get it over with."

"I can't understand you two," Holly burst out. "Before, you wanted to go—why don't you now?"

Judy actually shivered, though it was not too cold a day and she had her jacket well buttoned up, a scarf wrapped over her head and around her neck.

"It isn't the same," she said in a flat tone.

"Why isn't it?" Holly was growing angry. "We went with you and it was all right. Now it isn't right just because I had the dream, is that what you're trying to say?" She would not allow herself to be shaken by the thought that this was indeed her own doing, that she had not played fair last night. Because she was *right,* they had to warn Tamar of what was going to happen.

"Don't you care about Tamar at all?" she continued in a rush of hot words. "We can tell her—"

"But the bad men never hurt Tamar." Judy made no move toward following Holly in the direction of the wasteland which was the maze. "She and her house—they were gone—"

"Yes," Crock said slowly. "And where did they go? Do you suppose Tamar did know something—something about time? You know, people are beginning to think more about using their minds—like the TV show on E.S.P."

"Don't you see"—Holly seized upon Crock's speculation, whether she believed it or not—"Tamar must have known, or she and the house wouldn't be gone! So she was warned. And we're going to warn her right now—today!"

"But if it all happened 'way back like that"—Judy still stood her ground—"then how can it be that we warn her *now?*"

" 'Cause we go back in time—we must." Holly had questioned this herself over and over, and it was the only explanation which made sense. "We go back from *now* to *then.* We tell her, and she is already waiting to do whatever she did to save herself and the house when that old Sexton Dimsdale came."

"It could be," Crock conceded. "All right, let's get going."

Holly needed no further urging, she was already speeding away from the barn-house toward that tangled mass of leafless brush. As she approached the maze it looked almost as thick and solid as the walls of the barn. And it looked dead, too, gray-brown, as if there had never been any leaves on those entwined branches. At least not for years and years.

She had been watching for the tall cat guardians, but so far she had not sighted even a hint that such creatures had ever been fashioned of living growth. Her dismay began to turn to disappointment as she first trotted eagerly and then walked more slowly along the dead wall.

"There's no gate," she heard Judy protest. "I don't believe there's any way in now."

They were, Holly was uncomfortably aware, past the place where Judy and Tomkit had guided them before. Yet there was something in her which kept saying that there *was* a way, and that she would find it. She did not try to answer Judy, only went on around a curve where the wall itself drew back a little.

A moment later all her doubts were lost in triumph. "See there!" She flung out her arm full length, pointing at what was truly a break in the massed growth.

"Those—those aren't the cats," Judy said in a small, uncertain voice.

Holly surveyed the two guardians on either side of the dark opening. Judy was right, though Holly was not going to admit it openly. The creatures sat up in the same position that the cats had held, but they had no resemblance to Tomkit's species at all.

They were more than a head taller even than Crock and they had four legs, the hind ones curled under them for sitting. But their heads were a very strange shape— with long, pointed muzzles—while their ears were very

123 &

large and sharply pointed also. The gray-brown of the brush from which they were shaped gave them an unpleasant appearance, which was added to by some withered leaves clinging in patches, as if they were scaled.

"Alligators," Crock commented, and then added more doubtfully, "I think."

Judy stopped short. "I'm not going in there!" She shivered again. "This—this is not the right place at all."

"It is!" Holly stated determinedly. "I tell you—I know. Just as you knew."

But she herself was bothered by the look of those alligators, if Crock had named them rightly. The cats had been different. They had not seemed to be just waiting for someone to pass close enough so they could reach out and grab—that was silly! They were just some old dead bushes, the closer she went the better she could see that.

"Come on!" she ordered the twins.

Judy's face was very troubled. "I don't want to. Please, Holly, don't make me go in there. It's bad—"

"It's no more bad than your gate." Holly was thoroughly aroused to defend her own actions. "Just a lot of silly old bushes."

Crock reached out and took Judy's hand. His face was sober as he looked not at Holly at all, but at his twin. "We have to—now."

Judy sniffed, but she nodded unhappily. And Holly, to prove that she was entirely right, led the way. But she did not run eagerly ahead as Judy had done on that other exploration of the maze. She walked and tried not to feel how dark and closed in it was, and how the bushes seemed to bend down as if to catch and hold fast anyone who dared the very narrow trail between their dank, chill walls.

"You're going the wrong way. It is right—always to the right!" Judy said as Holly made her first turn.

Confident she had not forgotten that one small part of her dreaming, Holly shook her head. "No—it's left—I remember."

"Widdershins." Crock spoke and his one word echoed in that dark tunnel as if several people, all safely hidden, but still there, had answered him.

"What does that mean?" Judy asked. She held more tightly to Crock's hand and he appeared content to have it so.

"It's something out of the old times," he told her. "Widdershins means against the way the clock goes, against how the sun comes up and down. I don't know why I remembered that right now, but I do. There was something else"—he was frowning a little—"no, I don't recall that at all."

This tunnel did not take on any of the greenness of renewed leaves as they went, though Holly kept expecting it to. She hoped each time she made a fresh choice, and took another left-handed path, that they would see a change coming over the brush. However, though the walls remained starkly dead and leafless, there was a lower growth here also, and that thickened as they went.

There were toadstools, small at first, growing larger and more evil-looking all the time. Some were a dirty gray, and others were scarlet or spotted. There was a bright yellow one more like a thick finger. When Holly's boot brushed one of these, it popped open and there was a very bad smell. Other things grew, too, such as Holly

125 ❧

had never seen—queer grayish fat-leaved things which
had long stems rising from their center. These stems supported cuplike heads, which swayed in the children's direction as they passed, as if the plants could sense them.

The stone pavement underfoot was slimed, and small
nasty-looking fungi grew in the cracks between. To step
on one of these did not bring a good smell, but instead a
bad one. The children might as well have been in a pit
filled with garbage.

More and more Holly wanted to give up, go back. But
she would never admit that to Crock and Judy. Something
in her would not allow her to say that she was wrong,
that they must stop right here. Even when she tried, it
was as if her tongue could not shape those words.

It did not grow warmer as they went, either. On the
contrary, it was chill and damp, and they huddled deeper
into their coats instead of taking them off as they had
on their first trip through the maze. Holly stopped as
something moved ahead. It was as gray as the strange
flowers (if flowers these were) and it moved without a
sound. She gave a little catch of breath. Surely—that had
been a snake! Then it was gone, and she could not be
certain.

She tried to turn around, no longer ashamed of admitting that she was in the wrong, that they must get out
of here as quickly as they could. Then, to her horror,
Holly found out that she could not do as she wished, as
if something outside herself were pulling her on and on.

They came to another forking, a wider one. The pavement was sunken here and a muddy pool of water filled
the hollow. Looming above it was another of the brush
creatures. This was different from the guardians of the
gate, but its face was just as frightening, a face which

seemed very clear even with no leaves to round out cheeks and chin.

"I want to go home!" Judy cried out suddenly. "Crock, let's go home!"

Holly looked back over he shoulder. Though Judy was plainly upset, she had neither paused nor turned back. It was if that thing which was pulling Holly ahead held her sister also.

Holly heard Crock say unhappily, "I don't think we can, Judy."

"Why?" His twin's question was shrill. "Don't pull me like that, Crock! Let me go. I'm going back, right now."

"I'm not pulling!" Crock sounded alarmed. "Judy—I can't let go—honest I can't. You try—"

She must have done so without result. Her voice was even louder then as she cried out, "Please—I can't let go of Crock's hand! Holly, you've got to get us out—you have to! I don't believe this is the way to Tamar. She has good things, these are all bad ones. Holly—get us out!"

Holly tried to stop, to turn. But she could not. "I—I can't, Judy—something won't let me. It's making me go on—"

"Mom—I want my mom!" Judy cried, and then her plea became a helpless sobbing.

Holly had been afraid other times in her life, but she knew she had never been as afraid as she was now. This was a bad dream. Oh, please let it be just a bad dream! If she could only wake up—

There was another fork in the path with one of those horrible animals looking right at her. She saw big shiny places in the brush where its eyes should be. These were like mirrors. As Holly stared up into them against her will, she could see reflected there the three of them—

Judy crying, Crock looking very set of face, and herself—but small, very small. As if that big brush terror were so large it might reach out its upraised paw (for this one had one paw with long claws, too, represented by thick thorns, big as Holly's own finger) and smash them right down into the mud and slime under their boots.

Something very queer happened as Holly continued to look straight into those dull mirror eyes. First, she was not afraid anymore. What was there to be afraid of? Bushes and toadstools, one could see those anywhere at any time. And why was Judy crying? That was stupid, but then Judy often *was* stupid. Judy was a crybaby and she was jealous. She wanted to be the only one who could come into the maze and find Tamar. Now that Holly was proving how wrong she was, she pretended to be afraid, and wanted to go back. Sure, Crock was taking sides with her. He would—because they were twins and both of them always took sides against her, Holly.

Just look at them now in the nearest mirror eye. Why, she was big and clear and they were both small and misty-looking. She was the one who right from the first had had the idea about warning Tamar and making sure the witch was not caught.

She had been a little stupid herself about one thing. Of course a witch lived in the maze—a witch with the power to wish anything she wanted to happen. Just wait until Holly could have that power, too. And she could. Holly nodded to the big clear reflection in the mirror eye. She, Holly, could do anything—if she wanted to badly enough. Anyone could, if she worked hard enough and did not let anyone else talk her out of it. Like Judy and Crock had tried to talk her out of this.

No, she was right and they were wrong!

Without a backward glance at the twins, Holly turned away from the mirror eyes. Oh, they would follow, she smiled—they had to follow. The witch wish would see to that. And would they ever be surprised! Only she would not. She was Holly, and she was going to have some witch wishes of her own. There were lots of things she could think of wishing right now—things that would make Becky Eames and Martha Torrey sure wish they had never talked about *her!* Now Holly laughed as she thought of several very funny and unpleasant things a witch wish might do.

"Holly, please—don't sound like that!" Judy's voice was faint, as if it came from a long distance away. There was no use paying any attention to her. Judy did not know anything, she was a silly little girl, no bigger really than she had looked in the mirror eyes. A silly little girl of no importance at all. Holly made no answer.

She was walking faster now. Now there *was* a change in the walls, they were turning green after all. Why had she thought those toadstools and ghost flowers so horrible? Really, they were not. They had much more *character* (Holly chose a word she had heard Mrs. Finch use in that fashion) than just flowers one could see anywhere. Those toadstools were so big they must be the largest ones in the whole world.

The path made one more turn and here there was no brush animal to mark it, rather a tall stone pillar, and on the top of that a skull of some animal with great branching horns. The skull was half-covered with a greenish moss, but Holly had the feeling that it knew her, had guessed she would be coming, and was saying hello in an odd way inside her head, not so she could hear it with her ears.

Then she was out in the open. There was Tamar's house—just as she knew it would be. Of course, it was not summer, but you could see it even clearer with all the flowers and vines gone. And there was a steady coil of smoke from the wide chimney. But this time the door did not stand open—it was firmly closed.

Well, that was all right. Who was going to leave the door wide open on a cold fall day? Holly nodded to herself. You see, if you just thought about anything properly, you had the answer right before you.

The garden was just where it had been before. But now it was all dead, withered stalks of things standing here and there, blackened clumps of plants on the ground. It smelled dead, too, a nasty smell. But how else could it smell when it was dead? She must remember to think clearly, not keep comparing it in her mind with the other time she had seen it. That had been summer, this was fall. Grandma said things died quickly when they got a touch of freezing frost.

In the center of the garden was still the pool, and this had dull greenish-looking water. There was a dead bird lying on the rim, another floating in the water. What did that matter—they were only birds. People mattered. Animals and birds, they were only in this world for people to use as they pleased.

As Holly came along the walk, heading confidently for the closed door of the house beyond, something she had thought a big lump of frozen mud came to life and writhed away to the pool edge to splash down into the turgid water. A snake? No, she was not quite sure what it had been, and for an instant her step faltered. Then she remembered she was that big confident Holly she had seen in the mirror.

Nothing would happen to her. She was coming on a witch wish, and she was expected. What did she care for dead birds or a crawling thing in a dead garden?

In her mind there came a thought which was not hers.

"Well done, my brave poppet!"

How could someone "talk" into your mind that way? Still, the big Holly she had become somehow did not find this alarming.

"Better and better, my poppet!" approved the one she could not see or hear but who was talking to her. "Of use to my shaping, well chosen indeed!"

She was almost to the door when someone dragged her backward a step or two with a demanding pull at her arm. Hot with anger, Holly looked around.

Crock had her, and on the other side Judy closed in, both trying to keep her here from the door. What was the matter with them? They were mean, jealous! They did not want her to get the witch wishes. Well, she would—and when she did, just let the two of them look out!

A toad—she'd wish a toad to follow Judy around. To get into her bed—

"Splendid, poppet!" agreed the mind-voice. "And for this venturesome lad who would keep thee from thy pleasure?"

She—she would think of something.

"Let me go!" Holly cried out in a wild, angry voice. "You can't keep me from my wishes, you can't!"

"But Holly, look!" Judy was crying again, tears running down her round cheeks. "This can't be Tamar's house. Look up there on the roof! Tamar would never have *those* on her house. Look up there."

Holly's gaze reluctantly followed Judy's pointing finger. On the very edge of the roof above the door a row of small gray-white skulls had been fastened. Some were birds' skulls, she thought; others must be those of little animals. But what did a lot of old bones matter? They were only the signs of power—

"Just so, poppet, just so," agreed the voice in her head.

"Let me go!" She began to struggle against Crock and Judy's hold with all her might. She had to be free, to open that door, to meet face to face the one who had called her, to get her witch wishes so she could do what had to be done.

Holly did not quite know what she was to do, but it was very important and the time was short. If she could just get away from the twins. However, together they were more than a match for her, though she kicked out and tried to pull free. They were dragging her back—back away from the house. She must get free.

"Aye, the time for play be over." The voice in her head sounded louder, and as if it were a little angry now also. Then Holly saw the door of the house begin to swing open; it moved slowly, as if by its own efforts and from no real push.

Now that voice sounded in her ears instead of in her head, while Crock and Judy stood as if suddenly frozen, so that Holly knew they could hear it also: "In the name of Hecate, I bid thee enter—"

⮞ hAGAR

Holly went forward confidently without even glancing
around to see if the others were following. At first sight
this was the same house they had visited before. But the
woman standing by the hearth in much the same way—
she was not Tamar!

She was smiling gently, not watching the kettle before her, though her hand still moved to stir its contents with a long-handled spoon. Where Tamar had been plain of face and of clothing, this girl (for she looked much younger than Tamar) was very pretty. She wore the same type of cap, but it was pushed farther to the back of her head. Showing around her face were small curls of hair which were almost silver-fair. The wide skirt of her dress was green and it was kilted up over a second skirt of a darker green, while her long apron and the kerchief over her bodice were both edged with narrow plaiting, also of green.

The lighter green of her dress matched the color of her eyes. In her face these seemed very large, beneath brows and behind lashes which, in spite of the fairness of her hair, were dark. There was a dimple in her cheek as her smile grew broader.

"Good morrow to thee, my poppet," she said directly to Holly. "And to thy kin be it also a merry-a-day. Thou art prompt to the bidding, and that be in thy favor, small sister."

Holly stood tongue-tied. This was not Tamar. Then who was it standing at Tamar's hearth, using her kettle as if this were her home?

As if she could pick that question out of Holly's mind, the girl in green laughed, low and sweet. "Ah, be it that I know thee and not thou me, poppet? I be Hagar—"

It was not Holly who interrupted her then, but Crock. "Where's Tamar?" he asked. His voice sounded rough and almost too loud in the room.

Hagar's smile vanished. Her eyes narrowed, and for a moment Holly thought she looked like Tomkit when he was annoyed enough to flatten his ears to his skull and hiss a warning. But it was only for an instant that she looked so.

Then once more she smiled, and her voice was gentle and sweet: "La, young sir, my dear sister be abroad. I keep the hearthside this day, as thou seest. And thy company be most welcome, for this be a lonely place—"

"You're Tamar's sister?" Holly blinked. She was so unlike Tamar. But then Crock and Judy were twins and they did not look at all alike, either.

"Her sister, yes, poppet. But it be me thou hast come to see, be that not the truth?"

Slowly Holly nodded. Until this moment she had not been aware of that fact, but now she remembered a little of last night's dreaming. It had been Hagar, not Tamar, who had spoken to her in those dreams, shown her the way to come.

"Then let us have no more of Tamar. She has her own concerns, and this day we have no part of them but pleasure ourselves otherwise." Hagar laughed. "Ah, there be pleasures aplenty, poppets"—now she seemed to include them all as eagerly as if they were about to begin some exciting game—"which have not been known as thou shalt know them! But let me to the end of this labor and thou shalt see!"

She turned now to look into the pot, holding up the spoon and allowing the liquid to drip from it back into that seething below. The drops were a deep green color and fell slowly as if very thick. Now Hagar began to sing, softly and low, but so that Holly could catch each word:

> "Queen of Heaven, Queen of hell
> Send thy aid into this spell.
> Hornèd hunter of the night
> Work here thy will by magic rite.

*"By all the powers of land and sea
As I do say 'So mote it be.'
By all the might of moon and sun,
As I will, let it be done!"*

With the last word she tipped the pot, having reached behind her to the settle and from there picked up a basin. From the pot into the basin flowed sluggishly a thick trickle of the oily-looking green liquid. There did not seem to be much of it, though Hagar was careful to collect all she could, even shaking the spoon at last over the basin to coax down a few more drops which had clung to that.

There was a strange smell added now to all the others from the herbs and spices in the room. Holly could not say whether it was a good smell or a bad one. Just that it was like no other her nose had ever recorded.

Carefully holding the basin level, Hagar brought it to the long, cluttered table, setting it down beside a bottle in which was already fixed a funnel. Then with caution she began to pour the liquid from the basin into the bottle. She was so intent while she did this that Holly, without thinking, came closer to watch her.

The last drop filtered through the funnel. Quickly Hagar jerked it away and closed the bottle with a cork made of a rolled-up piece of bark tied tightly around with a green thread. She forced it into place and looked up with a smile.

" 'Tis done, and well done! With tasks behind, then playtime comes. What be thy will, poppet?" she said directly to Holly. "Wouldst thou learn what thy will can do when thou wouldst have such—?"

"Holly!" For the first time Judy spoke up. "Don't listen to her! Don't you dare listen!"

Once more that quick instant of anger changed Hagar's pretty face.

"Little one"—now she swung about a fraction to look beyond Holly—"thou hast a feckless tongue. Use it not too often lest it play thee false!"

"You stop it!" That was Crock. "You just stop frightening Judy!"

Hagar's eyelids drooped over those very brilliant eyes. She smiled again, but there was something secret about that smile. Holly stirred uneasily. Far down inside her, fear was sharp. Then Hagar looked up again and that secret smile was open and warm.

"Nay, lad, do not fear me. I will do thee and thy sister no harm. Contrariwise, I have much to offer thee. What be the dearest wish of thy heart? Think of it with all thy mind—"

"No!"

Hagar shrugged. "So be it. I do not offer twice, lad. Thou hast thrown away more than thou can guess."

Now she gazed at Holly as if both Crock and Judy had gone and only Holly were left. "But thou, poppet, thou hast learned well the way of the world. Take what thou wilt when thou hast the power. And thou shalt have that power—that do I promise. But also there be two sides to a bargain. I will give freely and thou shalt do freely."

"Do what?" Holly asked as Hagar paused.

The other laughed gayly. "Oh, it be little, so very little —for thee. But to me it will mean safety from those who come a-hunting. I know a little of what may lie hid ahead of me, and that little be enough. Thee brings safety, poppet; for that thee would be very welcome, but also for thy ownself. For in thee lies fertile soil for the planting—"

"I don't know what you mean." Holly was puzzled. She

could understand that Hagar wanted her to help in some way. But the rest of it—

"Thou shalt learn. It be in thee, and be now awake and ready. Dost thou not want to bring to others—" Hagar paused again. The tip of her tongue touched upper and lower lips. She did not add to that but smiled once more and beckoned Holly closer.

"Look thou"—her hands spread in a wide gesture which indicated the table and the many things upon it—"this be a school in which much can be learned. But only for those in whom lies the need. And in thee I see it. Thus I shall teach, and thee shall learn, when both of us be safe. But thou must make sure of that safety, my sweetling."

"How can—" Holly began, when they heard the singing outside, faint because the door was now shut.

> *"Lavender's blue, dilly, dilly!*
> *Lavender's green.*
> *When I am king, dilly, dilly!*
> *Thou shalt be Queen."*

"I shall be Queen!" Hagar caught up the stoppered bottle she had filled so carefully. "Oh, aye, I shall be Queen!"

She ran lightly around the end of the table, and was at the door. Holly turned to watch her go, and now saw Crock and Judy back against the wall, their eyes wide, and frightened looks on their faces. But they did not move, or watch Holly, as she went to the edge of the high window to look out.

She reached forward to brush aside the hanging leaves of a plant in a pot on the sill. Thus her fingers touched one of the small panes, which of itself went open on hinges, giving her a chance to hear as well as see what went on outside.

Seth Elkins came swiftly along the path through the frost-blasted garden. He wore a long cloak and a hat with a broad brim and a high crown. But that did not hide his face, and he was laughing a little.

"Ah, sweetheart, come thou to me as eagerly as I hunt thee out!" He opened his arms as if to take Hagar into them. But she was laughing, too, and drew back a step or two, eluding him.

"Be not so eager, brave one," she said. "Would thee put to naught all I have so carefully wrought for our future?"

She was holding the small bottle in both hands, and seeing it, he stopped short.

"Then thou didst do as thou threatened," Seth Elkins said slowly. All his open happiness of a moment before was gone.

Hagar drew back another step, frowning. "Why say thou 'threatened'? I promised that what could be set right for the twain of us, that would I labor to do. And thou did say 'Aye' to that. Why dost thou now use such a word to me who be thy true and only love? Or be it that thou hast come to terms with thy father and will go courting where he bids?"

"Thou knowest that be not so!" he said angrily. "Thou art indeed my true and only love. I go nowhere else a-wooing. My father's anger dost not move me into the road he would have me follow. But——"

"But?" Hagar repeated with a sharpness Holly had not yet heard in her gentle voice. "So there be a 'but'—explain it to me."

"What thou hast said—it be witchery."

"Witchery? What is witchery?" She flung up her head and stared into his eyes. "Dost thou name me 'witch'? If that be so, say it abroad—to the Reverend Eames and his like. Send me to my death and stand to watch me hang, as thou must surely do. I have no harm in what I do here, I am a healer and one who wishes all good to others. If thou wouldst incline thy father's mind to thee, then I can aid thee. That be what I promised; that be what I will do, if thee wills it. I mean him no harm—would I be so foolish? Already they whisper against Tamar, who be a fool, as many times I have told her. Should I add to their whispers by any deed of mine?"

As she spoke she went toward him step by step, her eyes still holding his. On the young man's face there was a queer look now which Holly did not understand, as if he could see only Hagar in all the world, and that what she said was all he could hear.

Hagar now held the small flask in her left hand. Her right one she reached forth, pushing aside the flap of Seth's cloak, resting it palm-flat against his chest. "Am I a fool, Seth? Am I one to give all those who have reason to wish us ill proof that their evil thoughts are the truth? Am I, Seth?"

"No!" He caught and held her tight. "No, Hagar, thou art my own dear heart and all the world to me. There be no evil in thee!"

"Remember that," she said. "Now, if it be thy will, this I shall pour forth upon the ground right willingly. For though it would serve us to our fortune, yet I will not have thee believe I meant any ill to a living soul!"

She had freed herself from his hold and now stood apart, her right hand upon the stopper of the bottle as if she would jerk it out and then do just what she had offered.

For a moment he looked from Hagar to the bottle, then back again. "What be in it?"

"Herbs only," she answered promptly.

"Then why should it incline my father to put aside his wishes and favor us?"

"It will soothe his ill humors, and he will be more ready to listen to thee. Look you—would I do this were I pressing upon thee some evil potion?"

Hagar did jerk the stopper from the bottle now. She held that between thumb and forefinger and plunged the little finger of her other hand into the narrow neck of the vial until its tip met the green liquid. When she withdrew it, a drop of the oily green substance clung to her flesh. Promptly she sucked that finger clean. Deliberately she replaced the stopper.

"See what I have done? Dost thou believe me now?"

"Aye." His hand went out slowly and she put the bottle into his grasp.

"How—when do I use it?" he asked hesitatingly.

"Three drops within that posset he does take when he seeks his bed. That posset my good sister hath given him to relieve his aching of the stomach. Do it so for three nights, then wait one, and then again for three. Thee shall see, over the days between he shall warm to thee as he has not since Master Dimsdale did ask thee to wed that squint-eyed daughter who be all he has for an heir. Three plus three, even as I tell thee and we shall be man and wife!"

"Hurry that day!" Seth was laughing again. He put the bottle into his pocket and then he swooped forward, caught Hagar under the arms, and swung her off her feet into the air, still laughing, while she was laughing, too. Then he kissed her.

But at length she pushed out of his hold again. "Be off with thee, bold one. Let not Tamar see thee, for she be jealous that I am courted and she be not. Trouble can she make. Also, that Patience Dimsdale does match her name: She slinks about ever watching and waiting. And until thy father's heart be turned to us, we want no roaring of Master Dimsdale. He hast been unfriendly to me for long, and to add logs to the fire of his anger would be indeed stupid. Soon shall it be, dear one, that we shall stay together forever—"

"May that be soon!"

As Seth went, Hagar stood there smiling, and she waved her hand twice as he half turned to view her. When he had disappeared she came quickly into the house, and Holly, feeling uneasy, pulled away from the window.

"What be done be well done," Hagar said, as if to herself. "If any question rises—ah, my dear sister then shall have the answering! Fool, thrice fool that she has been and will ever be!"

Her eyes fell on Holly and she nodded. "A new lesson to be learned well, poppet, though thou wilt not yet understand its meaning. Now let us make merry together and be as good comrades-in-arms—for such are we to be."

As Tamar had done, Hagar cleared one end of the table, moving swiftly and surely, setting out plates, bringing tankards and brown bread and honey. But this time Holly did not feel in the least hungry. And she saw that Hagar had put out only two plates, two tankards.

Holly glanced back at Judy and Crock. To her surprise they had not moved since she had seen them last, standing there against the wall with their faces set in those looks of surprise and fear. In Holly, for the second time, that fear of her own stirred once again.

"What—what have you done to them?" she demanded shrilly.

Hagar was tearing apart the small loaf of bread, dividing it between their two plates. "Thou art afraid, poppet!" Concern sounded in her voice. "But thee must not be. Fear causes a weakening of purpose, a slowing of thought. I would harm none of thy kin-blood. But they see ill in me and would do ill in turn to thee, for they have no understanding of that which lies within the two of us. Now it be as if they sleep. They shall remember naught except as a dream, very faint and without meaning. But thou shalt remember all, and also what must be done by thee. Now come, we shall eat together, for friends we be and friends share food and drink."

Holly went to the table very slowly. Sometimes it was as if, when she blinked, she saw another room, another person: not Tamar, no—but not Hagar, either. When that happened, for a flash of a moment she was afraid. Then that vision vanished and she was all right again and knew that what Hagar said was the truth and all was going to be well.

As Holly sat down on the bench, Hagar pulled up a stool to sit across the table from her. She raised her hands and made a sign in the air over both the bread broken in two on their plates and the liquid in their tankards.

Holly reached for the bread. She was not hungry, she did not want to break off a bite the way Hagar was doing and put it into her mouth. But with Hagar watching her so closely, she felt that it would be very impolite, or even mean, if she did not.

Unlike Tamar's bread, this had a dry feel on her tongue and very little taste. She had to drink quickly in order to swallow it at all. And the stuff in the tankard did not have the flavor the cider had had either, but left a tart stinging in her mouth.

"I'm not very hungry," she said, somehow unable to take any more of the bread, or drink that which left her mouth still burning inside.

"Nay? But I thought it was a kind of hunger which brought thee here, my poppet. Wert thou not a-hungering for that to confound thy enemies and bring thy own will to pass?" Hagar's eyes caught and held Holly's with that same searching as she had earlier used with Seth.

It was almost like looking into those mirror eyes which the strange brush animal in the maze had shown. Holly thought she could see herself in the green ones Hagar turned upon her, and as she did, her uneasiness vanished. Of course, Hagar was right! She wanted to learn the witch wishes, to be able to stand up for herself, to make them all sorry— She had not quite sorted out yet the "them" she wished to use her wishes against. But she would know, when the time came, she would know!

"Aye, poppet, thou shalt know." Hagar nodded. "But such knowledge comes not all in one moment or the next, mind thee. It grows as does a seed placed in soil which pleases it best."

"Are you really Tamar's sister?" Holly was not quite sure why she asked that question, or why Hagar's answer had importance. She only felt that it did.

"Thou hast doubts? Why? Because she be so plain of face and I be the comely one?" Hagar raised her hand to fluff the curls on her forehead. "Because she be older, and I young? But it be so—we be of one blood. Of one learning also—with powers. But now I tell to thee a small secret, poppet." She was smiling, her green eyes sparkling as if they were not eyes at all but glittering stones. "Aye, a secret, do and undo—she be not as wise or strong as she hopes, my dear sister. What she may do—that can I undo, as easily as I so snap this." She had picked up a long twig from the table top. Between her fingers it broke with a crack that somehow sounded very loud in the room. "What she would build, that shall I also bring to naught. Nay, rather thou and I together, poppet."

"Tamar—she was kind—" Again Holly did not know why she said that. But the words awoke in her a memory. Tamar—she had come here to warn Tamar of Sexton Dimsdale's plan! But if those men came to burn the witch house, they would also be enemies of Hagar.

"Listen—" Holly leaned forward against the table. Now that she remembered, she was doubly eager to give her warning. "Back there, where I—we—come from, they said that on Halloween Master Dimsdale and some other men, they came to burn down this house—kill Tamar—you—"

Hagar had not been mentioned in Grandma's story, but she was in just as much danger if she lived here.

"Back there, from whence thou comest—" said Hagar slowly. She either did not believe Holly, or else some other thought was more important to her now. "From whence dost thou come, poppet? . . . Aye, through the dream maze did I find thee. But I knew not the place in which thou wert, only that thou hadst worked the charm to open the gate between us. Now—tell me of thy world!"

She once more fixed Holly with her eyes—she might be seeing straight into Holly's mind, so direct and searching was that stare.

"It—it's different in time—I think." Holly added those last two words because she was honestly not sure. "It's nineteen-seventy in my world."

"Nineteen-seventy," repeated Hagar. She pushed aside the plate before her, dipped her fingertip in the liquid still in her tankard, and began to draw lines on the wooden table top, her head bent a little as she studied them with the same searching as that she had used when she had asked the answer from Holly. "So be it!" she said at last. "A different time. But tell me more—much more!"

Holly tried, but how could you tell all about the Dimsdale that was now, the world that was now? Such telling could take days—

"Dimsdale ruined, used to hold the castoffs." Hagar laughed. "What might Master Sexton say to that now? A good ending for a pride-filled man! But this world of thine—much has changed, that I can see. Only people, within them they do not change. And with people will I deal, with thy good help, poppet. Thou hast told me of trouble to come, and for that I am in thy debt. But when that trouble comes—Hagar shall not be here! Well did I judge to summon thee."

"But Tamar—" Holly ventured.

"Tamar?" Again Hagar laughed. "Did I not say that she also has power—of a sort. A pale shadow to the power she might hold were she of a braver heart. Let her fend for herself, as I shall do in my own behalf. I look forward to seeing with my own two eyes, poppet, this strange world of thine."

"You mean—you'll come back with us?" Holly was surprised and again uneasy. She did not see how they were going to explain Hagar if she did choose to come. And somehow she did not want that to happen. Hagar—

Tamar—they were part of something which, she suspected, should not be mixed with the real world, the safe world of the barn-house, of Mom and Grandpa and Grandma, of school and—well, just everything Holly had always known.

"Now that I cannot yet do, poppet. There must be a gathering of power. But safe I can be here, by thy aid. And the warning thou hast brought, that was well done. But thee can do even better: Make sure that this"—she made a sweeping gesture to include their surroundings—"be protected."

"How can I do that?"

"Easily, poppet. I shall show thee. And in thy nature there lies that which shall aid thee."

She arose gracefully from the stool. "Now do thou bide still while I gather that which must return with thee. And do thou listen well to all that I say. Thou comest to warn, thou wilt go surely to save."

Hagar went directly to a cupboard at the darker end of the room and slipped its heavy latch. Holly could see, within, small jars and bags arranged on its shelves. It would seem that Hagar herself was not quite decided which she would need, for she touched this packet, that jar, sometimes took one from the shelf and weighed it in her hand as if she must make very sure she selected that which was of the utmost importance.

At length she returned with several packets, one much larger than the others, but well wrapped so that Holly could not see what it contained. As she laid them down one by one on the table she spoke a name aloud, her finger still resting on each packet so named as if she were making sure Holly would know what it was.

"Furmentory, bryony, hemp; vervain, mugwort, moonwort, mullen, and the greatest of all"—she touched last the longer packet—"root of mandrake. Planted these must be, and in such a place as they may flourish unknown for a space. Dost thou understand?"

Holly nodded. Grandma's part of the fix-it shed. But now she asked, "What are all those for?"

"For our profit, my poppet. For as they grow, so will time be tied to time. Also wilt thou begin to grow in power. Moonwort—when it be ready—that thou may dream upon. True dreams such as those that brought thee hither. And when thou dost so dream, then shall I speak to thee and tell thee what thou must do next that this danger thou hast spoken of may not come nigh. Does thee now understand?"

"Yes." She could really understand that Hagar needed this help if she were to escape Sexton Dimsdale. And if Hagar escaped so would Tamar, too, Holly assured her uneasy conscience. Because this must be why the house and the witch were gone the next day after the men had been frightened away.

Hagar leaned forward, her arm outstretched. "Close thy eyes, poppet!" she ordered.

Confused, Holly obeyed, and felt a light touch on each eyelid.

"Now thy mouth." Holly, her eyes still closed, set her lips tightly together.

"As I do say—so mote it be!" she heard Hagar pronounce. "Well enough, poppet. Thy eyes shall serve, thy lips keep silence—until we meet again. And now, take that which must be set to grow, and return to thine own place."

She had put the packets into a bag of green, the green of grass or of fresh leaves, and this she handed to Holly.

"Judy—Crock—?" Holly asked uncertainly.

"They shall not remember, naught but that ye all have been lost in the maze. Lead them by the hand and they will come safely out of it. Thou shalt do very well, poppet, very well indeed."

Holly stuffed the green bag inside her jacket. But, as she was turning away from the table, Hagar spoke again. "Thy kin, poppet—thou hast brought them here, and what they have seen and heard—that was not for them, for they will not have it so. I have said that they shall not remember, and that be so if—"

"If?" Holly stood very still; there was something in that word "if," as Hagar said it, which chilled her.

"If thou dost what must be done, all will be well with them, for the fault in their memories will not then heal. But if thou choosest not to do—" Hagar shook her head slowly. "Then I cannot say what fears will haunt them. For thou, poppet, have seen things here as they are. But thy kin have not had that clear sight and they have seen what will be ill to remember, shall haunt dreams."

Holly looked from Hagar to Judy and Crock—their set faces. Yes, she could see fear there. Hagar was right. It was her fault that they had come, her fault if they would have bad dreams and memories.

"I won't let it happen!" It had been partly their fault, too—this came into her mind. But she would see that all was right, she would prove that *she* had been right.

"Just so, poppet. Remember all I have told thee and do what is to be done; thus all shall be well with thee in every way." Once more Hagar raised her hand and made a sign in the air.

Holly blinked. Had there been a strange glow about the other's pointing finger when she moved it so? Now it was gone and she was not at all sure she had seen it. She crossed the room and took Crock's hand where it hung limply by his side. It felt cold, as if he had been holding a piece of ice, and Judy's was the same.

Before them the door began to open slowly of itself. Leading the twins, Holly walked through it. The gloom outside was darker, clouds hung heavy over their heads, and there was a wind so chill that when it struck Holly full-face, it made her gasp. Home—just let them get back to the barn-house, where it was warm and everything was just as it should be! Crock and Judy came along, but they still stared straight ahead. Holly had heard of people walking in their sleep—was that what the twins were doing? At least they were coming and she could lead them easily.

They were through the blasted garden. Holly paused and glanced back over her shoulder, why she did not know. The door was shut again, there was not even a curl of smoke from the chimney now to show that someone did live there. But the house itself—Holly's eyes seemed to blur, and through that blur she saw the outline of something which was not like the house at all, but far more seeming to be a dark monster crouched and watching her with mirror eyes.

The impression frightened her so, that she plunged ahead directly into the gate of the maze, her heart beating faster. Her booted feet slipped on one of the slimy paving blocks and she nearly fell. Go slow, there was nothing behind her—

Down one way, turn, down another, always leading Crock and Judy. Now she was back with the monster who had the mirror eyes—she was sure this was the one. Only there were no shining disks in its head now, just big black holes. Holly shivered as she hurried by with the twins.

It was so cold, so very cold! And dark. Down near the ground in the tangle of brush, among the monster toadstools and ghost plants, were small specks of light. Holly saw them move, watching her—eyes! Eyes of things! She wanted to see no more of them, only be out of here, away into a world she could understand.

Turn, turn, and turn again. It would be so easy to make the wrong turn, only something deep in her mind *knew*. The eyes were growing bolder, she saw the ugly outlines of heads—rats! Holly gave a sound close to a whimper. She hated rats. But as yet none of them came directly into the path.

"Holly—Holly, where are we?" Crock suddenly jerked back against her pull. "Where—"

His eyes were no longer set in that sleepwalking stare. But he turned his head from side to side and he was still afraid, she could read that in his face.

"We're in the maze," she answered shortly.

"We've got to get out!" his voice echoed, as the terrifying eyes crept closer to the edge of the pathway ahead. Holly glanced down and then looked away again quickly. She was certain that other things besides rats were closing in upon them. But Hagar had promised—

It was as if remembering Hagar's name made the fear retreat. Crock—there was nothing for him to be afraid of, she thought with a touch of scorn. Why, he would never have come this far if she hadn't brought him. And they had nothing to be afraid of, Hagar had promised—

"Come on," Holly said harshly. "We can get out easy."

But Crock had turned to his twin. "Judy? What's the matter with Judy?" Now he gave Holly an accusing glance.

"She's all right! She's—she's sort of asleep. Come on!"

Crock shivered, but he moved forward, and now he had caught Judy's other hand and they drew her along between them.

"Tamar—" Judy's voice was hardly above a whisper.

Hagar had said that they would not remember, that they would only think they had been lost in the maze. If that was so, she, Holly, must be very sure not to say anything to make them know more. Because—Hagar had said it would be bad if they did. Now she tried to choose words to satisfy Judy.

"We didn't find Tamar—we just got lost."

"I don't like this place," Judy cried. "I want to go home. I don't want to be here!"

"We're going," Holly told her. "We're going just as fast as we can."

"But we're lost—you brought us in the wrong way, Holly; you knew it was the wrong way!" Judy's mouth took on a stubborn set. "I'm not going to go any way you say. We'll only be more and more lost—"

"No—look there, Judy—I remember this." Crock hurried on to the next division of paths. "Sure, it's this way."

Judy pulled her hand out of Holly's and sped after him. For a moment Holly watched them go. She was cold outside, and she was cold inside, too. Judy, Crock, they acted as if they did not want to be with her any more.

What if they don't, said something else, you know more than they do. Hagar—she said that you had the power, they didn't. Holly did not know what that "power" might be. But thinking about it made her straighten up and feel an importance she had not known before. She pressed both hands against her chest and the bag within her jacket. Do what Hagar said and she could learn more and more—then just let Crock or Judy say she was wrong! See what would happen then!

8 Second Planting

"Well now, an' what do you think of that?" Grandma
must have heard them come in, but she did not look
around from the table. She had leaned back in her chair,
was studying what stood before her.

The statue woman was whole. And she was—

Holly shook her head at her own first thought. Of course, that could not be a statue of Tamar! But it was of a woman who was dressed just like her, wide skirt drawn up on each side to show an underskirt almost as full, the apron, the collar, the laced bodice, and a cap covering most of her hair. Though the figure was all white, with no color to bring it to life.

"That's Tamar!" Before Holly could stop her, Judy had gone to the table and was gazing, fascinated, at the figure. "That *is* Tamar."

Now Grandma did look around. "Tamar—an' who's Tamar? That's a queerish name, to be sure. Wherever did you hear that one?"

It was Crock who answered while Holly still stood in dismay. "She heard it in an old story about Dimsdale. Tamar was supposed to live here once."

"That so?" Grandma was interested. "Somethin' Miss Sarah told you at the library, I suppose. Well, this here doesn't say no Tamar—let's see—" She pointed to some words at the foot of the base on which the repaired figure stood. "Now that says—" She stooped a little to see the better without having to touch the figure, holding her glasses very firmly in place as she did so. "Well, did you ever now!"

"What does it say?" Judy crowded closer, her own head strained forward. "Oh, look—there's Tomkit, too. Right down by her feet. It says"—Judy read the words aloud slowly—" 'The Young Witch.' That's a lie," she cried out. "Tamar's not a witch! She's good!"

"Judy!" Grandma spoke more sharply than she ever had to any of them before. "I did wrong in telling you all that there story of Miss Elvery's, that's plain. There ain't no such things as witches, 'cept in stories. Miss Elvery was so old, an' she had had so many troubles in her life—well, she didn't think too straight anymore. She read so much 'bout the old days, half the time she was livin' in them, rather than here an' now. I don't know about this here Tamar, but don't you go talking witches an' such."

"They hung witches at Salem," Crock broke in. "We saw the witch house where they had the trial. People did believe in witches then."

Grandma looked beyond Judy to her twin. That displeased note in her voice was even stronger as she continued, "They never hung no witches here." She looked back at the figure she had repaired, but now there was no sign of satisfaction or pleasure in her face as there had been earlier. "An' this here statue is jus' what some person thought up for hisself." She reached out for an old torn pillow slip (the one in which she had so carefully kept the broken pieces when she was working with them), and this she drew swiftly around the mended figure. "This goes out. Does Mr. Correy want it, he'll be entirely welcome!"

As she wrapped the figure she was still frowning. Then she arose and took it to the stall with the mended china, setting it down at the far back of the shelf. She might even be wishing now that she had not mended it or that it was no longer in the barn-house at all.

"That *was* Tamar," Judy said in a low voice, her eyes still fixed on the table from which Grandma had lifted the statue. "And it said she was a witch! Something bad's going to happen to Tamar—I know it!"

"No, it won't!" Holly had not loosened her jacket; she still held her arm protectingly across her middle, feeling between it and her chest the bag Hagar had given her.

Judy was really silly—just a child. Hagar was Tamar's sister, even though she had hinted that she did not like her much. But it was Hagar's house, too. And she would not let old Sexton Dimsdale burn it down. Hagar knew how to stop him—

Only she had made very clear that she needed Holly's help. Holly had to plant what she had been given. She could not understand how planting things in pots was going to help, but she was confident that Hagar knew, or she would not have told Holly to do just that.

Judy never looked around, nor did she answer her sister. Again Holly had that queer feeling, as if Judy were behind a kind of glass wall. She could see her sister, touch her, hear her, but Judy just was not close anymore.

Well, who needed her? A surge of confidence gathered in Holly, sweeping away her bewilderment again. No one needed Judy, but Hagar needed Holly. What she did was going to be very important indeed. And she must do it soon.

Grandma was inspecting other broken things along the shelf. She might be choosing another piece to try her skill on. Judy had turned away from the table, was heading up the stairs. And Crock was just going out the door. No one was watching, no one would come snooping around if she went right now.

Holly felt a small shiver of excitement as she slipped out behind her brother. Only one thing could spoil her plan. That would be if Grandpa was working in the fix-it shed. But Crock was not heading in that direction; he was going around to the other side of the barn where the driveway was.

Holly scuttled along the bare flower beds, where a few stalks, dried and dark, still stood, reminding her of the garden in the maze. The clouds were almost as heavy and bleak-looking here as those which had been hanging over Hagar's house.

She had her hand on the latch of the shed door when she jumped at a loud blast of sound. Someone was blowing a horn, a car horn, on the other side of the barn. Did that mean that Grandpa was in the shop and he was being called? Holly pulled the door cautiously open.

No, the workbench had some tools laid out there, and on the floor stood one of the old trunks they had brought from the Elkins place, its lid off. Maybe Grandpa was trying to fix it. But there was no one here.

Holly slipped through to the green side where Grandma's protected plants stood in their rows. She pulled the bag out from under her jacket and went down on her hands and knees to peer under the table. Yes, she was in luck, there were more empty pots there. She had to crawl under the table to pull them out, but she got them.

Spider webs—ugh! Holly wiped her hands down her jeans. She hated spiders, they made her feel all crawly when she saw them. But Grandma did not believe in killing them, ever. She said that they caught a lot of bugs as had no business being in houses and annoying folks.

Now, Holly remembered, she'd have to go outside and get the dirt, as she had before. That was going to be risky. The one window of her and Judy's bedroom looked out in this direction. What if Judy saw her and wanted to know what she was doing? But Holly did not see how else she was going to get those pots filled.

With the basket and trowel, she went out quickly. No one was around. A glance up at the window—the curtain hung straight there. Better not take any more soil from the flower beds. It was more risky walking toward the maze out in the open this way, but she was sure she could dig up more at a time from along there and no one would notice it.

Holly worked as fast as she could, but the ground was hard and there were tough grass-roots and stones. She dug with energy, all the time alert to any sound. That car horn had stopped blowing, but now and then she thought she could hear voices. Mostly they seemed to come from the direction of the old cellars Grandpa had filled up with the unusable junk. It was his plan to get as much of the waste inside those cellars as he could and then floor them over with rocks so they would look better. It was like his planting trees: He wanted to keep Dimsdale looking as nice as he could.

But who could really make a dump look like anything but what it was? Holly used the point of her trowel like a pick to loosen up the tough clods. This dirt did not look very promising, but it was the best she could do. Maybe she could get some of those plant vitamins they sold at the dime store—the kind Mom had fed her African violets. Those would make up for not having any good soil. The point was she had to plant the things Hagar had given her—plant them and hide them, as quickly as she could. Without anyone learning about them.

For she was as sure as if Hagar had openly warned her that no one must know she had brought these seeds and the long, odd-looking root back from the maze. If Crock and Judy never remembered what had happened in Hagar's house, she was safe.

Holly now thought of the place in the maze as Hagar's house, though they had seen Tamar there, too. Only Holly found it increasingly difficult to remember Tamar very well. While she could close her eyes at any moment and see Hagar as clearly as if she were standing right here watching her dig holes in the exceedingly hard ground.

The results of Holly's digging were discouraging. When the soil was dumped into the basket it was all in hard lumps. Maybe once she got it inside she could break it up, even use one of Grandpa's hammers to mash it if she had to. To add to the difficulty of the digging, Holly felt she had to keep looking around to make sure no one was watching her.

At last the basket was almost full to the top, and when she lifted it, the weight was nearly more than she could manage. But she tugged it back to the shed. There was a pile of newspapers in one corner. Grandpa spread them on the floor when he was painting.

Holly grabbed some of these and put them down, set the basket on top, and began to ladle the lumps into the pots with her trowel. Perhaps coming into the warmth of the shed made them break apart. Because even the largest began to crumble, and a few energetic thumps with the trowel broke them up completely. She had to scant on the last two pots, but she was afraid to·trust to luck and venture out the second time for more soil.

Seeds went down into the soil as quickly as she could shift them in. The biggest pot had to hold the root, and she arranged that in the pot with all the care she could, using her hands to build up the dirt around it.

Now—Holly squatted back on her heels and surveyed the shelves. She and Judy had hidden the other pots; she must do the same with these. Only she could not see too much room left. Standing as tall as she could, she began to move those already on the shelves, wedging in one of her pots well to the back wherever she could discover the necessary space. Finally only the pot with the root was left. Holly could see nothing else to do but to push it well back under the table, hoping that it would grow in spite of the dark—at least get a start.

While she pushed and changed the other plants around, she was surprised to see that at least two of those Judy had planted showed a tiny slip of green breaking through the soil. There was no way of telling which these were. For they had not thought to try to mark the pots with the seeds as they had put them in. Holly could not even now clearly remember the listing of those Tamar had pressed upon them. Nor did she care now. The important ones were indeed those *she* had brought back, though Hagar had never quite explained why they were so needful.

Holly was careful in her cleaning up. Judy might sneak in here to see what she had planted, Grandma certainly often visited her winter garden. No one must guess, at least for now, that Holly had made any additions. She looked around at last with a sigh of relief. She had done what she promised, and she would get the plant vitamins the first chance she had. Those ought to help a lot.

As Holly left the fix-it shed she was as careful to look about to see if Crock or Judy were spying on her as she had been when she entered. They had no right to try to find out about her business, hers and Hagar's. Cautiously she pushed open the barn-house door, trying to think up some possible answers to any awkward questions that might be asked.

"—you can see their way of thinkin', Lute. 'Course, no one can say you don't do the best you can to keep it in order. Only this is a dump, and Mr. Reuther, he says he'll pay top price. Judge Tanner, he's lookin' into the hassle with that Mr. Porter Dimsdale out west. Seems like he ought to be glad to have it all cleared up. The thing's been hangin' on long enough. I jus' came out to let you know how it stands, Lute. We would be doin' nothin', but them new people, they got up and made a fuss 'bout a dump being close to 'em and as how this needs clearin' up to make the town look better 'fore the celebration.

"Now don't you take it, Lute, that any of us we're sayin' as how you ain't doing a bang-up job here, 'cause you are. But there's jus' so much you *can* do 'bout a dump. An' if this Mr. Reuther means what he says—"

"Then"—that was Grandma, speaking sharp and clear —"you'll have you some more streets with all them little houses what looks 'zactly alike, an' no trees nor nothin' —jus' all bare."

"I guess so. There's more'n more folks as want to live out away from the cities. And they've got to go somewhere."

"They don't live outta the cities," Grandma countered. "No sirree, they jus' brings their old cities 'long with 'em when they moves. How long we got, Mr. Bill, 'afore these new city folks want to roust us out?"

"Can't tell, Mercy. It's gotta come up 'fore th' town meetin'. And that over-the-river crowd, they do a lot of talkin'. I jus' wanted to warn you straight off that there may be trouble waitin' right 'round the bend. Now me, personally, I don't want nothin' to do with this Reuther fellow. He talks big, but I want to see if his doin' comes up to his talkin'. Dimsdale place was a big fine house once. Pity that burned. Were it still standin' we could take it over for show, jus' like they did the old Pigot place, and these people what are fixing up the Elkins' house are plannin' on doin'. But nowadays, it seems like they just want to sweep away everything from the old days, was it good or bad, they don't care. Well, I'll be gettin' on. Thanks for th' snack, Mercy. That was right tasty raisin pie. Seems like you get more taste in your cookin' than most of the women 'round here who do a lot more boastin'.."

"That's right kind of you to say that, Mr. Bill." Grandma did not sound happy when she answered, but more as if she were worried or upset.

"You got any ideas as to what they's goin' to say at the town meetin', Mr. Bill?" That was Grandpa.

"Only just what I've been hearin'. Lotta talkin' goin' on. There's some—Jim Hooker, and Ira Batchler, they listens when the new folks talk. 'Course Jim, he runs the garage and Ira's got the hardware. Them two, they are makin' money offen those allotment folks. Seems like them houses o' theirs, they always need a mite of fixin'. And you know that Ira and his boy, they go out on their own doin' a little carpentry here, a dab of plumbin' there. And the garage gets about twice as much business now that the development is open. It ain't, I guess, that Ira and Jim are against keepin' things as they have been, they's just wantin' any pickin's they think might be comin'.

"As I see it the main trouble's that Mrs. Stanley Deevers, her and her bunch of know-it-alls from the other side of the river. She tried to push into the Ladies' Thimble Society over to the church and tell 'em how they needed to wake up and do something more up-to-date. Only when Mrs. Pigot stood right up to her, she got miffed. Then it was the school board, and we heard a lotta talkin' as to how our school's so backward no young'un is like to get any education." Holly heard a rich, hearty laugh follow that. "Was she ever caught with one foot in a mud-puddle when Dr. Peabody pulled out that record book of his and started to point out the number of scholarships and such our young'uns have been winning.

"Mrs. Deevers, she tried to say as how our school was so backward, that we didn't teach nothin' about livin' in this here today world. But she didn't get too far with that there foolishness. People is too proud of the school, and they got a little hot about her sayin' all that. So she calmed down a mite and we didn't hear her argyin' 'bout things for a spell. Then she turns up with this new idea —'Beautiful Sussex,' for the Tri-centennial. And the trouble is, Lute, Mercy, there she's got ahold o' somethin' as don't bother people so. They ain't goin' to get their dander up defendin' no town dump from Mrs. Deevers. Then, with Mr. Reuther comin' in and hintin' as how he'd be right willin' to take it over and develop it—well, money talks, even though he's really plannin' to make it into a lot of little tacky-lookin' houses as nobody but city folk, who can't see further than the end of their noses, is goin' to buy. But me, I got one darn good question I'm savin' up for town meetin' (that's comin' on November tenth): I'm goin' to rise right up and ask do they take away the Dimsdale dump for a development, but where then is they fixin' to put the trash next? Pitch it out alongside the roads, maybe? What kind of a beautifyin' kinda thing is that goin' to be? That's just what happened over to Norfolk—and that's what came of it, too. You'll hear me sayin' enough to make 'em think. If those dumb-between-the-ears fellers *do* think. We can give 'em a fight do we want to. Me, I'm goin' around right now tellin' it like it is to enough of the old-timers as can throw some weight around. I had to warn you, Lute, Mercy, but we ain't got to the fightin' part yet—and me, am I goin' to give 'em a whale of a fight!"

Holly heard the other door slam, and now she slipped fully into the warmth of the barn. Grandma was sitting at the table, her hands spread out on the top, and she was looking at Grandpa right over the tops of her glasses, which this time had nearly slipped off her nose though she did not seem to notice.

"Luther, whatever in the world can we do?" That voice did not sound like Grandma's at all, but was thin and wavery, like the voice of an old, old lady.

Grandpa was by the door, as if he had just seen their recent visitor out. "Do, Mercy?" He swung around and his voice was not thin and wavery at all, it was hard. "We gonna do jus' what Mr. Bill Noyes said—we're gonna fight!"

"But he said, an' he's right, nobody cares about a dump. That can be just anywhere—"

"Nobody cares 'bout a dump?" Grandpa was still fierce. "Mr. Correy—where's he gonna get his antique things? And Lem—he does a lot with his repaired stuff. And Mrs. Dale—the Scouts, they need the dump for their projects. Miss Sarah at the library, who'll see she gets all them old books? Twice now, ain't we found things as she said were the best she ever saw? That there journal of Seth

Elkins as she shows around every time there's new people at the museum, who found that? You did, Mercy, right here at this dump!

"An' it ain't going to be all dump, neither. Ain't you an' me, Mercy, ain't we been workin' plantin' things an' tryin' back there"—Grandpa waved his arm energetically at the wall behind Holly without looking at her at all— "to make it look good again? There's all yore herbs an' such as you is known to have. Things like none of them garden-club ladies ever seen 'afore. Didn't they say so last year when Miss Sarah had you over to th' library to tell all 'bout 'em? No sirree, Mercy, I tells you plain they ain't gonna sweep us an' Dimsdale away so easy. Put up them little old houses as gets outta fix quick as a family moves in 'em an' try to spread out a little—"

Grandpa's face was flushed, and he shook his fist in the air, Holly thought, as if he dared one of the development houses to sprout up in the middle of the barn like one of the big mushrooms Holly had seen in the maze.

One of the big mushrooms. Holly gulped. What had Hagar promised? That she could teach Holly how to to make wishes come true! She had done what Hagar had wanted. Now Hagar would have to keep her part of the bargain. Holly would wish, and that Mrs. Deevers, who-ever she was, would stop meddling—

In the moment Holly forgot that she hated the dump. It was hers—or rather it belonged to Grandpa and Grandma, and she was living here. Now she felt as fierce as Grandpa looked. No one was going to take Dims-dale and run bulldozers all over it—cut down the maze—

Cut down the maze! But if that happened, how could she ever find Hagar again and claim her wishes? No, no bulldozers in the maze!

"When is the town meeting?" Holly asked.

Both Grandma and Grandpa gave a start and looked around as she came out of the shadows behind the last stall and walked toward the table.

"Where you come from, Holly?" Grandma frowned at her. "You been listenin' without us knowin'?"

"Yes. I heard that man talking." Holly was too full of what might happen to notice Grandma's frown very much. "How soon will we know—about what they plan to do?"

"This ain't no bother for young'uns." Now Holly was aware of Grandpa's very unfamiliar sharpness.

But Grandma was shaking her head slowly. She did raise her hand now and push up her glasses, but she did that as if she were very tired, and not with her usual emphatic thump. "You can't keep young'uns from knowin' somethin' like this, Luther. They'll hear the talk soon enough in town. We don't know nothin' for sure, Holly. An' until we do, you don't say anythin' even if you is asked. You understand?" She gazed at Holly in a way which was a warning Holly could not disregard.

"Yes," Holly answered. She longed to say that Grandma and Grandpa need not worry, if she could just get to see Hagar again. But when could she?

If she tried sleeping on the pillow again tonight, would it work? It must! She must get to Hagar as soon as she could. Or maybe—Holly shivered—maybe Hagar would do nothing unless the plants grew out there in the shed. And it might takes days before they showed. Get the plant food, she could do that; she had enough money left from her allowance to buy at least one package.

She wanted to go up to her room, get out her purse, and count how much money she had left, because she had bought that special notebook for her project yesterday and she was not quite sure now. This was more in her thoughts at present than Grandma.

Grandpa had reached for his coat, which was hanging up on the end of one of the stalls.

"I'll put the truck under cover tonight," he said. "There'll be a stiff freeze by all the signs, if I know 'em."

Grandma jumped up. "Freeze—an' m' plants in the fix-it shed. Where's my coat, an' my scarf?"

"Now don't you take on, Mercy. I'll see to loadin' up the stove. No sense in you tryin' to do it. That old stove never did work good for you nohow."

Holly, who had frozen herself at the mention of the plants, relaxed when she saw that Grandma was not insisting on seeing to that chore. As Grandpa went out the door she headed for the stairs, intent on two things. She must find the pillow and make sure she did not forget where it was so she could use it again to see Hagar. For by now Holly was convinced that the pillow was the real key to the maze. Then she must also portion out her money to get the plant food which would coax the seeds she had planted to grow as quickly as possible.

When she got to the bedroom she expected to find Judy, but there was no sign of the younger girl. Holly went straight to Judy's box of cloth pieces, which was in the wardrobe. Moments later, with its contents all on the floor about her, the box turned upside-down and empty in her hands, she knew only one thing. The pillow was gone. And there could only be a single answer—Judy had taken it!

Which meant that unless she could get it back, she would be unable to meet Hagar—to get those witch wishes!

"She's got to give it back!" Holly kicked angrily at those treasured squares of Judy's, all those pieces she was saving up to make a quilt when Mom had time to show her how.

The trouble with Judy was that when she got an idea into her head it was set there for ages and ages. You could not change it by talking to her, not in the least. Just as she had been planning her quilt for almost a year and she never forgot about it or lost interest.

But just now those pieces around Holly's feet did not matter in the least. What did was that maybe Judy had some ideas about the pillow. Could she even have destroyed it?

Holly moved back and sat upon her bed with a desolate thump. If Judy had done that—how was she ever going to get to Hagar and claim her wishes? And if she did not, what would happen to Dimsdale?

9 Dimsdale in Doubt

"My pieces! Holly Wade, did you do this?" Judy, her eyes snapping in anger, stood in the doorway of the room.

"What did you do with the pillow?" Holly did not heed these signs of one of Judy's very rare outbursts of temper.

"My pieces!" Judy repeated. She was down on the floor crawling around now, picking up, smoothing out. "Holly, this is about the meanest mean thing anybody could do! You're plain *mean*!"

But there was only one thought in Holly's mind. She caught Judy by her shoulders, giving her a vigorous shake. "You've got to tell me! What did you do with the pillow? It isn't here anywhere, I've looked."

Judy twisted hard enough to break Holly's grip. Her lower lip stuck out and she gave Holly such a hostile glare that for a moment the older girl drew away.

"Won't tell you! Everything's gone wrong since you took that pillow, Holly. I found your draw piece of paper, too. And you are a cheater! It was really Crock's turn and you grabbed it. Then what did you do, you took us in a place and lost us! You're not going to do that again, Holly—me an' Crock—we're not going to ever let you. You had no right to dump out all my pieces like this. I'm going to tell Grandma, ask her if I can have my own room where you can't pull my things around. So there!"

"You don't understand," Holly began—then it was as if something stuck in her throat. She found to her surprise that she could not say what she wanted to: tell Judy about the wishes; and Hagar's promises—the need to get help for Dimsdale.

"I understand just how mean you are!" Judy exploded. "And I don't like you anymore, Holly. Ever since we've come here, you've been getting meaner 'n meaner. You're just like an old witch yourself! So there!"

Judy was in her most stubborn mood. Holly fought her own impatience. Something bubbled up in her; she wanted to hit Judy, hurt her, *make* her tell where the pillow was. Then—Holly sat down on her bed. What made her want to hurt Judy? She had never felt like that before in her whole life. Oh, Judy could be stubborn and hard to reason with at times, but never before had Holly had the impulse to hit her, hurt her so hard she would have to do as Holly said. What was happening? Holly knew a growing fear she could not explain, nor did she really understand what she was afraid of. Unless it was that wild part of her which wanted now to strike out—to hurt—

She huddled miserably on the bed. This was like being two people all at once. One was the Holly she had always been, and the other—the other was someone she was afraid of. She *had* been mean dumping Judy's pieces all out on the floor—

Holly stooped to pick up the nearest, only to have Judy snatch it out of her hands. "You just let that alone! You let all my things alone after this. You let *me* alone, Holly Wade."

Holly sat down again. Maybe if Judy knew about what was going to happen to Dimsdale— She wet her lips. Would she be able to tell about that, or would she find she could not tell, as she had not been able to tell about Hagar?

"Listen, Judy—" she began.

Judy turned her back on her sister. She was busy now, restoring her pieces to her box. "Won't!"

"Judy, this isn't about the pillow, it's about Dimsdale, the barn-house—everything. You've got to listen, because it's important." Holly kept on talking to Judy's back. At least Judy was still in the room, and her ears were not stopped—she just had to listen.

Holly repeated what she had overheard, and what Grandpa and Grandma said afterward. Judy had stopped putting her pieces away. Now she faced about, the anger gone from her round face.

"What are we all going to do, Holly?" she asked slowly.

"There's this meeting, a lot of people don't want it to happen. But this old Mrs. Deevers, whoever she is, she wants to do away with the dump. And somebody called Mr. Reuther wants to buy the land here to build a lot of new houses."

"He can't," Judy said flatly. "Tamar won't let him! Tamar won't let them take Dimsdale away from Grandma and Grandpa."

"Judy, you know Tamar's not here. She lived a long time ago."

"She's here, you saw her your own self," Judy declared. "And she—she loves Dimsdale."

Holly stared at her sister. Judy's calm certainty surprised her.

"Tamar—she's not real," Holly began again, not quite sure just how to find the words to impress Judy. How *could* you say that a person was not real when you had been in her house, eaten her food, talked to her?

"I don't mean she wasn't real once," she corrected herself. "But she's not real now. We *must* have gone back in time to see her, Judy."

"I say she's real, and she'll help us!" Judy's stubbornness was back. "You are just saying that because when *you* tried to take us to Tamar we never got there! I'll bet Tamar didn't want to see *you!*"

Holly's desire to prove Judy wrong, to tell her that they had gotten to the heart of the maze a second time, was so strong it actually choked her. However, again she could not say the words; again something prevented her. Holly now believed that Hagar had more power than

Tamar. Hagar—she would help. But she could not get to Hagar without the pillow, and she was well aware that she would get nothing directly from Judy as to where the younger girl had hidden it.

"No"—Holly chose her words carefully—"we didn't get to Tamar. But we ought to, we ought to tell her about Sexton Dimsdale—before Halloween. And we ought to tell her about what may happen now, see if she can help us."

Judy gazed at her sister thoughtfully. "Maybe—" But she did not sound sure. "I'll think about it. Only next time there's not going to be any cheating about the pillow!"

"Yes." Holly was ready to promise anything. Though she knew that if she could only find the pillow—and she was sure it was not in their room—she was not going to be bound by that promise. She was going to try to get to Hagar!

When they went down for supper, Grandma and Grandpa said nothing about their visitor of the afternoon. In fact they talked about things in the future exactly as if they were always going to be right here in the barnhouse, and nothing would happen to it.

"You young'uns been thinkin' 'bout yore dress-ups for the party?" Grandpa asked, as Grandma started to pile the dishes together. "There's prizes, you know. Them what gets the most unusual costume, or fancy or whatever, they get the prizes."

"I know what I'm going to be," Crock announced almost before Grandpa was finished. "A robot. I'm going to get me some of that heavy foil and make a regular robot suit. Got a picture—look here!" He took out his Christmas wallet and from it took a picture cut from a magazine, passing it over to Grandpa, who held it quite close to his eyes as if he did not want to miss a single detail.

"A robot, eh," he commented. "One o' them walkin', talkin' machines as they think we is gonna have to do all our work in the future. Ugly-lookin' cuss—"

"But I can make a suit like that out of foil, can't I?" Crock wanted to know.

"Need somethin' a mite heavier'n foil, I opine," Grandpa announced. "Think maybe, was we to put our heads together, we could cook us up something. Take a look-see 'round tomorrow . . . And what about you, now?" He looked to Judy and on to Holly.

What did any old Halloween costume matter? Holly thought. She didn't even want to go to any old party, but she supposed they'd make her. Ought to dress up like a piece of junk—maybe—

If Holly had not made up her mind, Judy was firmly set on her own plan. "I'm going as a cat, a cat like Tomkit, not a black one but a gray one," she said with the firmness of somebody who did not intend to be argued out of her choice.

"A cat—hmmmm—" Grandma looked at Judy and then at Tomkit, sitting on the hearth, washing a hind leg with a great deal of attention. "Black cats are usually for Halloween—"

"Like Tomkit," Judy insisted. "Holly says it's too hard to make a costume like that, but I'll bet you could do it, Grandma."

"Gray—" Grandma seemed to be thinking. "Well, now, I jus' remembered 'bout that old blanket—the hairy one. I think as how that could be dyed gray. Then they do have cat masks in the dime store. Those I seen last time I was in. That'd be black, though, not gray."

"Maybe you could paint one gray," Judy said eagerly

"Don't know about that. But we can try. You gotta remember that Halloween is gonna be cold. We have to have anything you young'uns wear big enough so underneath you got room for sweaters an' jeans. Otherwise you might take your deaths of cold. Well, we got us a cat, an' a robot. What are you going to try, Holly?"

A thought had suddenly flashed into Holly's head, she did not know how or why. "I'm going to be an African princess." She could do it, she had that *djellaba* Mom had made her from the brilliantly colored piece of material they had found on the remnant table last year. It looked as if it came from Africa or some far-off place. Her hair—yes, she knew just what she was going to do about her hair. Something she had wanted to do for long time, but Mom had said she wasn't old enough. It was *her* hair, wasn't it, and she could do it by herself. She had watched Eva Lee Patterson do hers often enough back home. She could get some big hoop earrings at the dime store, and wear a couple of long bead necklaces.

"I've got the costume already," she continued. "Mom made it for me last year."

Grandma nodded. "That's good, Holly, 'cause there won't be much time for fixin', an' I'll have to bend my mind a little for this cat suit Judy wants. Now, Luther, I got to get into town tomorrow anyway. Mrs. Jeffries has ordered all them special candles for to send to her daughter, an' I got me quite a few odds and ends o' shopping to do. So when you run in to drop that side table at Mr. Correy's, you can just take us along. That one little bit table ain't gonna crowd up the truck so much we can't pack in. Then you can pick us up at the Emporium 'round noontime. How's that sound?"

"You sure, Mercy, you all be through shoppin' by noon?" Grandpa laughed. "All right, it sounds to me like somethin' which can be did."

After the dishes were washed, Grandma brought out some newspapers and started measuring them against Judy, slashing them up with her big scissors here and there as she worked out a pattern for a cat suit. Grandpa and Crock were prowling around in the stalls, hauling things around. Holly sat on the settle by the fire, watching. She tried to coax Tomkit to come and sit on her lap but he ignored her, firmly hunching down on the hearth, his eyes fixed on the fire as if he saw something of absorbing interest in the flames.

Putting the cutout papers to one side at last, Grandma went to an old box against the wall and pulled out a queer-looking blanket (if blanket it was) that had long hair fastened into its weaving, more like one of the pieces of fake fur people used now for rugs.

"Mohair," Grandma said. She unrolled it and began to lay her newspaper patterns here and there on it, changing them around to take advantage of every bit of the blanket. It was a yellowish-white and there was a big stain of yellow right in the middle..

"It'll have to be a dark gray now," Grandma pointed out to Judy, "seein' as how we got to cover up this here stain. An' you'll need a bit of wire or somethin' in the tail part to make it stand up a little an' not just drag along."

"I knew you could do it!" Judy's eyes were shining. She hugged Grandma impulsively.

"It ain't been done yet, child." Grandma smiled. "But if it can be done, we'll do it."

Holly had a lonesome feeling. With it, she was unhappy. How could Grandma, Grandpa worry about an old Halloween party and act as if making costumes for it were important? What was important was maybe saving their home and getting back at people like this Mrs. Deever who just went about making trouble for everybody. When she got her witch wishes—she'd take care of Mrs. Deever. Her thoughts made a wall between her and the others. Was she the only one who cared—who wanted to *do* something? If she could only make Judy understand about the importance of getting back to Hagar! However, if she could not talk about Hagar, then she would have to use Tamar—insist again that they warn her about the trouble on Halloween, use that as a talking point to make Judy produce the pillow.

When she had worked that out, Holly felt relieved. Why had she not seen that way of doing it before? Judy would listen if she was careful about saying she was afraid for Tamar.

But there was nothing she could do about it now, not until she got Judy alone. Holly was bored watching Grandma and Judy, Grandpa and Crock—all so busy. With even Tomkit ignoring her, she was alone. She could plan tomorrow about shopping at the dime store. There were things for her to buy, if she had the money. Holly suddenly remembered that she had not, because of the scene with Judy, emptied out her purse to see just how much of her allowance was left.

Upstairs was cold. Grandma brought up hot soapstones to put in each bed when they went to sleep, and she said soon they would move downstairs. They could clean out some of the stalls and those would be bedrooms. Also Holly knew better than to light the candle which was kept beside her bed for emergencies: Grandma had warned them about fire.

"Now that's all we can do tonight, child," Grandma said to Judy as she cut out the last piece of pattern for the cat costume. "Tomorrow when we get home I'll boil me up a mess of dye an' we'll give this blanket a good dousin' in that. Has to dry then, an' it'll shrink some. But we can still get out what we need, I'm certain sure o' that. Time's gettin' on, we'd best start bedward."

Judy was very full of the cat costume and her need for a cat mask. She was sure there would be one at the dime store. Holly held to her patience as her sister talked. Put Judy's back up again and she would never get any help out of her. She dug down into one of the suitcases with their summer things in it, which Mom had said did not have to be opened now, to find the *djellaba*. In the lamp-light its colors looked brighter than ever—really cheery. For the first time she was rather interested in the thought of dressing up, though she was not looking forward to the party.

Holly was still undecided about when to approach Judy on the subject of Tamar, but she had no chance to argue further that night. For when she climbed into her bed, she was suddenly as tired as if all the unhappiness of this day had thickened into a sleep weighing her far, far down.

The next morning there was so much to do: Breakfast was followed by what Grandma called "slickin' up a mite." Which really meant making the living portion of the barn-house as tidy as they could. Then Grandma brought out the statue she had mended.

"I got me a funny feelin' 'bout this," she said as she

179 ঙ্গ

fitted it into a carton and stuffed old rags and dried grass tightly in around it. "First off, when I was workin' on it, I liked it—wanted to have it around. Now, I don't. I'll just take it to Mr. Correy, an' if he can make anything of it—so much the better!" She tapped down the lid of the carton. "Now let's see: There's m' candles, an' them jars of preserves an' pickles I set aside to let Mrs. Pigot have for the Emporium, an'—I guess that there's the whole of it."

The children were already wearing their gloves, jackets, and caps. Grandma put on a coat with a fur collar, which fitted very snugly up about her chin, and a knitted cap almost like theirs.

"T'ain't fashionable, I know," she stated as she fastened the tie ends, which pulled the cap well down over her ears, under her chin. "But m' ears don't take kindly to the chill. Better to be comfortable than cold any day!"

Holly and Crock volunteered to go in the back of the truck: Holly taking on the responsibility of seeing that the carton holding Grandma's repaired statue suffered no injury, Crock keeping an eye on the other carton with the jars of jam and pickles. It was bright and sunny, but there was a strong wind. They sat with their backs to the table Grandpa had lashed in with rope, pulling over it and them the tarpaulin to keep out the force of the wind.

Holly was very glad when they reached town. They did not stop at Mrs. Pigot's (Grandpa would do that on the way back, to leave the carton), but kept on down the main street, pulling up in front of a small building Holly knew from their class's walk across town had once been a combined blacksmith's shop and livery stable. This was Mr. Correy's antique shop now, and he came right out almost before the truck stopped.

He was a big man, towering over Grandpa, and did not

look in the least like an antique dealer, in Holly's private opinion. More like a farmer or one of the men working at the lumbering camp. She had often seen them drive through town.

"Good to see you, Luther, Mercy!" he rumbled in a voice as big as he was. "Saves me a ride out to give you an order, Mercy. I've got it written down for you—whole set of candles for the Livingstones. They got some this summer and wrote back that they want more. Come in—come in."

While he and Grandpa, with Crock standing by to help if need be, got the table unloaded, Grandma and the girls went inside. Holly was afraid to move around much. The room was so crowded with things, things she believed would break easily and cost a lot of money. Every table, the shelves of tall china cabinets, the tops of old desks, had cups and saucers, little figures, vases. No one could even see it all, it was just as crowded as Tamar's house.

Grandma had taken the statue carton in by herself and now was loosening the top as Mr. Correy came over to the end of the room where there was a big old desk with just piles and piles of papers and notebooks messed on top of it.

"Now what kind of a treasure have you got for me this time, Mercy Wade?" he asked.

"It came out of the Elkins place—in th' trash," Grandma said as she loosened the packing around the figure and began to pull it out. "Thought as how it might just be one of them Rogers' pieces you were talkin' 'bout. But I don't rightly know. It was broken pretty bad—but I did get it together."

"Even restored, when you do it, Mercy, it's well worth showing," he said. "Here"—he swept a lot of the papers into a single pile and made room on the desk for her to set "The Young Witch" in plain sight.

"There you be." Grandma brushed a last wisp of straw from the kilted-up skirts of the figure.

Mr. Correy just stood and looked at it, his eyes a little narrowed. "If it is a Rogers'," he said slowly, "it's a new one to me. Might be somebody trying his hand at the same kind of folk sculpture. 'The Young Witch.' You know, Mercy, that face now, it might almost have been done as a portrait."

Now he took it up carefully and ran his hands over it. "Marvelous job, Mercy, just like you always do. I tell you—Halloween's coming on—we'll just trim up a season display in the front window and make our young witch the center of it. Leave it on consignment as always, Mercy?"

Grandpa nodded. "You do your part of the business in your own way, Mr. Corry. To tell the truth—that there's somethin' I'm glad to see the back of."

"Why?" he asked curiously.

"Can't say. Just it gives me shivers a little. I get a feelin' like some old sadness was a-peckin' at my mind tryin' t' make me 'member somethin' I'd do well to forget. Well, an' here's the mornin' wastin'. You jus' give me that list of candles now an' we'll be on our way. We've got some shoppin' to do."

"Right here"—he flipped through the pile of papers. "Yes, here it is. She'd like them before Thanksgiving, she says."

"She'll git 'em, providin' all goes well." Grandma hesitated. "You heard 'bout the Meetin', Mr. Correy? How they is sayin' Dimsdale is an eyesore as has to be gotten rid of?"

He frowned. "I heard. And they're going to hear from some of us on the other side—don't you worry about that, Mercy. We're getting up a counter-petition that will make that Deever female think a bit."

"That's good hearin', Mr. Correy. 'Course we won't never know how a wind is blowin' till it hits. But I'll get you the candles, whether or no, anyhow."

The dime store was much further along Main Street, in that section where there were newer-looking buildings, a drugstore, a restaurant, and some other stores. All these had a big modern signs which somehow looked too bright and a little trashy. Only a small section of the street touched the park with its two statues, one of a Revolutionary soldier and the other of a Union Army man, who faced each other over a pyramid of cannon balls and the cannon which maybe had once fired them. The houses around three and a half sides of the park were all big and old, most of them painted white, with white wooden fences marking off their front yards. At two corners stood churches, and at the third was a big building toward which Grandma started out first. That was the old posting inn, almost two hundred years old, and it was where they would deliver the box of candles Crock now carried.

10 Blight

Holly sat with her project notebook before her. But for a
good ten minutes or more she had not made any additions
to the lines she had already written there. What she had
put down was all Grandma and Grandpa could remember

about Dimsdale in the days when Miss Elvery was still alive and they had come to take care of her and the run-down property.

"Things, they was in such a mess as you couldn't believe, didn't you see them for your ownself," Grandma had declared. "Miss Elvery was a lady an' she weren't never used to do hard work. She had a couple of girls. Girls? They was old women when I first knew her but they didn't have no other place to go, an' Miss Elvery kept 'em. Emma Watkins, she was bedfast an' Miss Elvery nursed her like she was close kin.

"Liza Peabody, she hobbled 'round doin' what she could, but that weren't much, I can tell you. As for the outside—lawsy, you had to cut a path in like they do in the jungles you see in the *Geographic* pictures, it was all growed up so much. There hadn't been a hand turned to keepin' it up after Miss Elvery's pa died an' she had to let Silas Hawkins go.

"We, Luther 'n me, had just got married an' we wanted a place to ourselves. There weren't none roundabouts as we knowed of. In those days, folks, black like us, we weren't welcome to move into town. It was better to keep to our own kind. But Miss Elvery, somehow she heard 'bout us, an' she came drivin' over with that old horse an' a broken-down buggy. She offered us the barn-house free an' clear o' any rent, and land for growin' things.

"Luther, he was workin' on the roads makin' cash money, an' with the barn-house an' a garden, we knew we could manage good. Then when I saw the mess up at the house—an' Miss Elvery never complaining about it neither, well, I pitched in an' did what I could for her.

"She began to teach me things, too—all about herbs. She had a garden of them, only things she tended outside. An' she said as how anybody could get learnin' jus' by tryin'. She lent me an' Luther books an' showed me all kinds o' fine sewin' an' the like. She treated us like we was friends an' neighbors. Emma, she died that first winter we was here. That was a welcome release for the poor old soul. An' Liza, she had a stroke. Fell down right in the kitchen an' only lasted a day an' night after that.

"So then I took over in the house. It was way too big for Miss Elvery, so we closed up a lot of rooms. She had her bedroom right off the kitchen. An' she used that for a sittin' an' dinin' room an' didn't try to keep up the rest of the house—'cept the library. Miss Elvery loved readin'. She read the same books over 'n over. Used to tell me how live the people in 'em seemed to her, like they was sittin' right in the room talkin' about all their troubles an' such.

"Once in a while she'd go through the house with me an' point out things an' tell me their history—good as readin' a book. Pity it was all burned up. She had things better'n in the museum Miss Sarah started at the library. Then she got the rheumatics, an' when it got cold she had to stay in bed a lot. But she was still alive in her mind, an' she read an' she quilted. Her piecework quilts, they's all burnt up too, they was like pictures they was so pretty. Never saw any to touch 'em.

"Luther, betweentimes when he wasn't on the road crew or gettin' a day's work on some farm, he went at the garden. We raised most all we ate. 'Cept meat. Come butcherin' time Luther'd give a helpin' hand for part of the meat. Miss Elvery—she didn't have no money, 'cept once or twice when she tol' me to sell something out of the house for her. She knew that the old things were beginnin' to interest the summer people. But she had to be hard-driven 'fore she did that. And mostly she used the money she got from that to help other people, too.

"She always worried 'bout the taxes, but she'd manage to scrape up something. Me and Luther, we'd add what we could. 'Cause we had the barn-house, you see. Then toward the end, Miss Elvery, she got lost in time, you might say. Her rheumatics got better, an' she'd think it was years back an' she was goin' to a tea party or the like. She took to wandering 'bout the house at night, huntin' something. Though she never made plain to me what it was. Then—well, she got in the old parlor an' she must have fainted like an' dropped her candle. Lucky I was comin' up to check on her when I saw the flames. Luther, he heard me screamin' an' he broke the window an' got Miss Elvery out.

"We brought her down here. There was no savin' the house, nor nothin', 'cause the town fire department was too far. We had no phone an' couldn't call 'em. Luther, he went runnin' down to the forks where the Wilsons lived. They called the doctor an' come back with him. By that time the house, it was gone. An' Miss Elvery—the doctor said her heart was weak. Though she lived for a little while here, she never remembered nothin' an' finally just went to sleep. She was a good lady."

Then Grandma had sat silent for a moment before she roused and added, "Make sure you say that 'bout her, Holly. She was a mighty good lady as worried 'bout others. Maybe people have forgot. I ain't, an' I never will.

"Then the lawyer, he came out. Seems she didn't leave no will—or if she did, it got burned up in the house. But he did have a paper she give him a long time before with the name of some kinfolk as went west years an' years earlier—after the Civil War, it were. He said he'd try to trace them down. Meanwhile, Luther, he had the paper Miss Elvery had given him when we first came to live here an' he showed it to the lawyer an' Sheriff Haynes. It said as how she wanted us for caretakers.

"They got together an' said we could live on here, an' then this idea of the dump started. The Selectmen, they put Luther in charge of that. But there was somethin' wrong about the old survey of the whole property—nobody could sell or buy it till that was settled. It seemed as if"—Grandma paused—"until right now, nobody cared."

By questioning, Holly had been able to learn what the Dimsdale house had looked like, and she had tried to draw out the picture, with Grandma there to tell her if she was wrong or right. Also she was able to learn about the big garden.

But when Holly had mentioned the maze, Grandma shook her head decisively. "That there's unlucky," she declared. "Miss Elvery, when we first came, she warned Luther not to try to cut into it any. Of course, we wondered why, it was so old and thick an' maybe full of snakes. But she was afraid of the maze—that I know, from the way she talked about letting it alone. She seemed to think that all the bad luck did come from inside it somewhere. I told you, Miss Elvery, she believed that her family was cursed an' the evil was in the maze—"

"Maybe the witch lived there." The words were out of Holly's mouth before she could stop them.

Grandma looked at her quite crossly. "There weren't never no witch! There was a girl as old Sexton Dimsdale wanted to git rid of so as he could have the land an' house. It was mighty easy in them days to say 'witch' an' cause someone a heap of bad trouble. I read a book 'bout what happened in Salem. They told lies 'bout good people as never did no wrong, and they hung 'em, too. It's mighty easy to tell lies 'bout people who are different, who ain't like other folks. We as got black skins, we should know that. Miss Elvery, she was too deep into them old books an' things in that house of hers. It made her believe when she had no reason to. Misfortunes, those happen to everyone, they ain't sent by no witch. A lot of bad things we bring on ourselves 'cause we have bad thoughts in our heads, or hate in our hearts."

Holly squirmed. There *was* a witch—at least there was Tamar, and Hagar, her thought added. And they *did* live in the maze. But she could not explain all that to Grandma. Now, as she finished writing out all Grandma had told her, and what Grandpa had shown her of what had once been the Dimsdale gardens, she still did not have enough. To get into the town library and see Miss Noyes, ask her about the Elkins journal she had shown them, that was the next important thing. But how to do it? They had not gone in on Saturday since two weeks ago when they shopped, and then Holly had had no time to visit the library. She could not go over after school or she would miss the bus home. She chewed the end of her ball-point pen and read over the little information she had gathered.

There was not much about witches, except Miss Elvery's story. Unless she dared set down their own experiences in the maze. If she did that, no one would believe they were true. Nor had she been able to persuade Judy to say where the pillow was. Judy spent much of her time tagging after Grandma, asking about herbs and how they grew, what they were for. *Her* notebook was fat already. And Crock was mostly after Grandpa. Sometimes Holly got so impatient she wanted to throw things, stamp and yell. But she knew that that would not get her the pillow; such actions would just draw attention to what she wanted no one to know. She had reluctantly decided she must allow Judy to think she had given up about the pillow. Judy might then let slip where she could find it.

Holly had never been so patient in her life. Usually, when she wanted to do something, it had to be done right away. But this time there was no other answer. She drew out a book she had borrowed from the library shelf at school. It was a story, not real history, but it was about the Salem witches, and she read it with care. There had been girls, just like her, or Judy, and they had started it all, accusing people of bewitching them. The book made Holly uncomfortable, but she had read it through.

That was Salem. This was Sussex. But there had been a witch hunt right here at Dimsdale. If she could only find out more about it!

She was still staring down at a page when she was aware that Judy was standing by her side.

"Holly!" Judy no longer treated her as an enemy, by now. But neither did she tell Holly everything she was doing, as she used to. "Holly, there's something wrong—"

Judy looked anxious and uneasy. She had on her jacket and cap, and Holly knew that she must have just come in from outside.

"Wrong—where?" Holly snapped shut her notebook.

"In Grandma's plant place. Holly, it's—it's bad!"

Holly sat very still. She had gotten plant food, dumped it into those pots where she had planted the seeds and the root Hagar had given her. She had gone in to water them at times. But so far none had shown signs of life.

And she was afraid that if they did not grow, she would have no chance to bargain with Hagar.

She did not dare to ask what Judy meant, but she must see. Now it took only a few moments to scramble for her own outdoor clothing, follow Judy.

"Grandma," Judy explained as they went out into the cold, "said she would let me water all the pots; I could learn about herbs that way. But Holly, I must have done something wrong!" Judy was very close to tears now. "They're all dying! They're turning yellow and looking funny as if they're sick. Do plants get sick, Holly?"

Holly was really afraid now. If Hagar's plants died, how could she ever make her bargain? What had Judy done to them?

When she demanded to know that, Judy shook her head. Tears were rolling down her cheeks now, and she made no attempt to wipe them away with her mittened hand. "I didn't do anything at all. 'Cept put water on them from the little can just like Grandma showed me. That's the truth, Holly."

When they entered the garden end of the fix-it shed, there was an odor which made Holly's nose wrinkle. It smelled a little like when you open a garbage can on a hot summer day. She could see the drooping plants: yellow and indeed sick looking.

"Tamar's things, they were just beginning to grow good." Judy gulped down a sob. "And they're dying, too. Grandma will think I did something bad, and I didn't. I just gave them water, 'zactly how she said to. Holly, what ever could have happened to them?"

But Holly was hardly listening. She was pushing aside pots in which things drooped and had lost proper color, looking for her own planting. Yes, there were shoots showing. And those were not sickly looking at all, but standing up well and healthy looking. She gave a big sigh of relief. So far, then, she was safe—

"What's that thing?" Judy had crowded closer. "What's that you're looking at, Holly?"

Without thinking, Holly answered. "One of those I planted. It's all right. What about the others?" She shouldered Judy out of her way to find the next pot she had hidden, and the next. In each there was visible growth looking both vigorous and healthy.

"*You* planted? Holly, what do you mean? Those Tamar gave us, I planted. And they were all in the red pots. I ought to remember, because I put them in just like she said. So where did you get something to plant?"

Holly was squatting on her heels by the table, peering under it at the larger pot in which she had put both the root and an extra helping of the plant food. There was a shoot almost as tall as her middle finger.

"Holly." Judy's hand closed pinch-tight on her shoulder, jerking her back so she overbalanced and landed sitting on the floor. "I'm asking you—where did you get those plants? Who gave them to you?"

Again before she thought, Holly answered. And this time she was able to say the name: "Hagar did. And Judy, they're all right. She said if they grew and were all right she and I—she said I could have witch wishes! I can get rid of that Mrs. Deevers and all those who want to take away Dimsdale—"

Judy was no longer crying. Her face was stern, set; in that moment somehow she looked just like Mom when Mom was angry.

"Who is Hagar?"

In that second Holly realized what she had done. But

why could she talk about it now and not before? she wondered fleetingly. That was not important, anyway. What was important was that Judy must understand how well her plan, this part of it, had worked.

"She's Tamar's own sister. Only she knows a lot more than Tamar—" she began when Judy interrupted her.

Now Judy's expression was one of fear. "We—then we did find the house—but Tamar wasn't there. That other was. She—she's bad, Holly—bad!"

"No, she isn't!" Holly's long-restrained impatience broke free at last. "You're just a silly little girl, a baby, Judy Wade. That's what you are!"

Judy was retreating, her eyes on Holly. She looked— Holly refused to believe that Judy was really watching her as she had watched the brush monsters in the maze.

"She's bad," Judy repeated, "and somehow—somehow she's making you bad, too, Holly."

"Judy!" Holly got to her feet but not in time. For her sister flung herself at the shelves, was snatching at the green pots, smashing them violently to the floor, so that the dirt flew all over.

Holly jumped to stop her. But her boot went down hard on one of the young plants and she skidded and fell again, bumping her head against the table leg in a way which made her feel very queer. Somehow, though she struggled, she could not get up again in time to stop Judy. One by one the pots thudded to the floor. Now Judy was trampling fiercely on the soil that spilled from them, stamping again and again at the plants, until they were just a mash.

With the aid of the table leg Holly pulled herself to her feet. She felt so queer, perhaps it was the bump on her head. Then, suddenly, when she looked at the mashed plants in the mess on the floor, it was as if something other lay there—nasty things, but mashed and helpless now. Judy was crying, but she still hunched down and reached under the table to jerk out the final pot. She upended it in the middle of the floor and then jumped with all her might on that crooked root and the small stem that had grown from it. When she had done, she stood, panting.

"Bad," she repeated. "All bad. And they killed Grandma's plants and Tamar's, too!"

Holly's head felt light and queer. She was dizzy and weak, as she had been once after she had the flu and got up and tried to walk and her legs were wobbly and had no really stiff bones in them. And—she felt empty. Not empty the way one does when one is hungry, but another kind of emptiness. She was crying, and she never knew she had started to, the tears just were there. While a choke in her throat hurt.

"You were helping the witch," Judy said slowly. "You really were, Holly. I can remember now. We weren't just lost in that maze, we found Tamar's house all right. Only Tamar wasn't there. That other one, she was. She's— she's the witch, Holly. Don't you see, those people— Sexton Dimsdale, the others—they thought Tamar was the witch. I'll bet that other one made them think so. And she made you believe it, too!"

Holly was shaking. She was sick at her stomach and her head was so funny. When she tried to see Judy, the room began to swing around.

"Hey, what're you doing in here? What a mess! And what's wrong with Holly?" Crock had somehow appeared.

"The witch got her," Judy said solemnly. "We *did* go through the maze, Crock, I remember it all now. Don't you? And that other one, she *was* a witch, a real one. She's got Holly and—".

"I'm going to be sick," Holly quavered.

"Come on!" Crock caught her by the arm. "Let's get out of here. I'll take you to Grandma. Judy, you'd better see if you can clean up this mess some before Grandma sees it."

Holly was sick, very sick, right outside the door of the shed. And her head was still swimming. She was hardly aware of Crock's steering her into the barn-house.

It was dark when she awoke again, to find she was on a cot near the fire. She was warm and then she was cold; her throat hurt, but her head did not feel so floaty anymore. Grandma brought a cup of something which smelled like herbs and had her drink it all. Then she went back to sleep.

There were dreams. She thought once she saw Hagar, only she wasn't smiling, she looked old and ugly, and Holly was afraid. Afterward Tamar stood there, nodding, as if all were well again. Following that, Holly did not dream, at least not that she could remember.

Grandma said she had the flu, but somehow Holly did not quite believe that. Though she had been sick and now she was getting better, much better. Privately she thought deep down inside that she had been sick ever since she took the pillow by cheating and everything started going wrong.

As soon as she had a chance to be alone with Judy, she asked: "The plants?"

"I cleaned up." Judy talked fast for fear Grandma would come back and hear. "Crock helped me later. We got rid of the bad ones. Now the rest are growing all right. Those others were poison, I guess, those you planted."

Holly moved restlessly in the nest of sheets and blankets. "She told me I was like her, a witch," she said in a low voice. "I guess I was acting like one. But I kept thinking what I could do with the witch wishes—help Grandpa and Grandma and Dimsdale. But mostly I was thinking about using those wishes to hurt people, too." It was hard for her to admit that. "Judy, what about Tamar—and Halloween?"

"We have been thinking about that. Crock and me," Judy replied. "I just bet that Hagar, she never told Tamar trouble was coming. We have to get back—"

"I can't go, not if I'm sick," said Holly from the depths of dark disappointment.

"Halloween comes on Saturday." Judy stated what Holly already knew. "The party isn't until four in the afternoon. Mom isn't coming that weekend again. If you used the pillow the night before—"

Holly shook her head. "No, I spoiled things when I cheated. You or Crock, you do it."

She was sure she would be well by Halloween, a whole week and two days away. And she set herself to the task of getting well. Nor would she agree that she would take the pillow again. Even if it came to her fair and square, she would be afraid—afraid that what Hagar had said was the truth and that there was something way inside her which would lead her the wrong way again.

Holly had a lot of time for thinking during the next few days. Judy came home twice with cards Holly's class had signed as cheer-ups. She studied these, picturing the person behind each name. They wouldn't have sent cards if they had really not wanted her in the class. It was hard to have to change ideas about people and things. But see how wrong she had been about Hagar. More and more she wondered how she could have been so very wrong. And what would have happened if Judy had not found and destroyed those plants? Yes, she had a lot to think about.

When Holly went back to school, she was shy at first. It was hard to change all around and try to talk to people. However, she could thank them for the cards. And, since everyone was talking about the Halloween party, that was something she could eagerly listen to. Also Mrs. Finch took them for a second visit to the library to work on their projects. This time Holly had a chance to ask about the journal of Seth Elkins. When she said she was living at Dimsdale and was writing about that, Miss Noyes allowed her to read the typewritten copy of that part of the journal which covered Seth Elkins' connection with the Dimsdales. Halfway through, Holly found a part that made her shiver:

This woman did give unto my good father that which she swore would heal the pains within his stomach. For a space did he seem the better, and arose from his bed and went cheerily about his business. But the second time she did make a potion for him, his pain did not ease, but became the greater, so that he suffered much. Master Dimsdale, chancing to come to sit with him one night, did question him closely. When my father did say he had the potion from the healing woman, Master Dimsdale became wroth. telling my father that he had dealt with a witch. He took up the bottle of medicine. Some he poured upon a piece of meat and this he threw to our old mastiff. The dog did eat, and shortly afterwards it had a fit, so that it was as if mad. Master Dimsdale did then take my father's pistol which was nigh to hand, and did shoot the dog dead. Having thus proven, as he said, that the witch did deal death to those she held in hatred, he summoned those of substance in

197 ❧

Sussex, telling the tale and showing them the dead dog. He did say to them that the following night being that one of evil repute known as All Hallows' Eve, that be the time to burn out this witch, destroying with her all which was hers, lest something of her fearful powers ·linger to plague us. So it was decided among the elders that this was right and proper for the preservation of all of us.

When it came to the next night we did gather, each man with a torch well aflame, and we went to that house where she dwelt. But I, knowing what was to be, had sent to H. a warning, for why must she suffer for that which was not of her doing. But T. was there, and she faced our company boldly, being doubtless strengthened by her lord, the Devil. They would have taken her and bound her, thrust her back into her den and set that to the flames. Only then there sprang out of the house devils such as make a man fearful to remember. And being afeard, all fled.

Master Dimsdale was not minded to be so frightened off, and at a later hour he returned, this time well-armed, having run forth silver bullets such as all devilish creatures cannot face. But when he came, and those others with him, there was no house there. But they did say that out of nowhere sounded a voice to curse the Dimsdales root and branch, saying that all would waste and perish until that which they had taken would be returned. But of the meaning of the latter words, none knew.

I did wait many days for H. to come to me as she had sworn, but she did not. Now I believe that that foul witch, who was no true sister to her, did so reft her from me. And thereafter I fell into a dire wasting sickness which Doctor Ashby could not understand. Nor have I ever been the same man since. H. being gone, I did follow my father's command and wed with Patience, though I have had no joy of that, nor ever will in this world, of that I am certain.

Slowly Holly copied it word for word. But this was wrong. Maybe Tamar had given the medicine, but Hagar had added something to it. And Seth Elkins had known that, only he did not mention it. Was that because he could not—just as Holly herself had not been able to talk about Hagar until Judy found the plants? What had happened to Tamar and the house? Halloween—it had happened on Halloween. If they could get there first— warn her! They must! But this time they must go the right way, reach Tamar and not Hagar.

ALL hALLOWS' eve

Grandma was busy most of Friday baking. She made
doughnuts, and cookies cut out with cutters Mrs. Pigot
lent her. These were in the form of bats with outstretched
wings, pumpkins, and cat heads. Holly and Judy helped

her finish after they got home from school, setting raisins in for the cats' eyes and using yellow frosting to cover the pumpkins.

Judy's cat costume was finished. Grandpa had wired the tail so it did not flop limply, but stood up the way Tomkit's did when he was setting out on his own affairs. Crock's costume was even more unusual. When he was fitted into it, and the square "robot" head placed over his own, he looked like something out of a TV program about outer space. He had to walk jerkily, too, because the pieces around his legs were stiff, and that made him seem even more a robot. There were curled wires standing up from his head, and he had small lights (red ones) for eyes (his own seeing through little holes beneath), which lighted up red, run on a little battery above them. Mr. Lem Granger, who came to the dump for electrical throwouts, had become quite interested in what Crock and Grandpa were fixing up and put in those eyes, showing Crock how to turn them on and off.

Though Holly wanted very much to cut her hair and brush it out into a regular Afro, she did not quite dare. But she unbraided and combed and brushed, using a small bottle of hair spray, until it stood out in a big fluff. Her robe was of the brightest colors: red, orange, green. With it she wore big hoop earrings and a lot of long necklaces. Some were made of painted pieces of macaroni, others of beads. After all, no one in Sussex had ever seen a real African princess, and Holly thought she looked like one.

She was smoothing out the *djellaba* as Judy came in. When Holly saw what her sister held, she sat down a little hurriedly on the bed. Judy had the pillow, and behind her came Tomkit, mewing and making small jumps at her feet.

"Crock and me, we're willing for you to take it"—Judy held out the pillow.

Holly jerked back. "No! I don't want it. Maybe Hagar was right, maybe I'm like a witch. If I take it we'll go the wrong way again. You or Crock—you take it."

"Crock says 'No,'" said Judy slowly. "He says he feels like he shouldn't try it. He's been keeping it an' when I asked just now, did he want a chance, he said 'No.' So—so I guess I'll have to do it."

She smoothed the upper side of the pillow. "I just noticed something, Holly. These funny lines, they're really like the path through the maze, with the breaks in them coming where you make a turn. They're different, one side from the other. On this side"—she traced a way with a fingertip—"they go with the openings to the right, just like we went to find Tamar. But over here"—she flopped the pillow over—"see here? These open to the left, like when you went to Hagar. Maybe you had the pillow wrong side up when you slept on it."

Holly took the pillow very reluctantly into her own hands to study those lines of stitching. It was true, she could see, as she reversed it once and then back again. Two ways through the maze. But she did not believe that it mattered which side was up when you slept upon it. What did—Holly had been thinking about this for a long time and was now sure—what mattered was how you felt your ownself. And she could not trust herself as she trusted Judy now.

"It's yours." She dropped it hastily on Judy's bed. "Are —are you afraid, Judy?"

"Maybe, a little. But we've got to go, to help Tamar. I know that is true, Holly. I don't know how we can help, but I keep believing that we can." She picked up the pillow, turning it carefully to the side where the paths all ran to the right, and settled it against her regular one.

Tomkit was purring so loudly they could hear him. He jumped to the bed, sniffed long and luxuriously at the pillow, and curled beside it, so his black nose just touched the very old and yellowed linen.

The girls climbed into bed as Grandma came for the lamp. "Big day tomorrow," she said. "You get a good sleep now, you hear?"

Maybe Judy did go to sleep. However, Holly twisted and turned under her blankets and the big comforter. Tomorrow morning they were going to clear out three of the stalls, Grandma said, move cots down there. It was getting too cold to use the rooms above. Holly listened to the queer creaks and groans which were always a part of the barn-house, and thought once she could still hear Tomkit purring. But there was no sound from Judy, and Holly did not want to wake her if she was already asleep.

Perhaps it was because Holly was awake so long that she overslept the next morning. It was Grandma's bell ringing which brought her entirely awake. Judy's bed was empty, the covers neatly spread up. Holly hurried to dress and to fix her own bed. She could see no sign of the pillow. Had it worked again? Could they go into the maze before they left for the party? Time—would there be enough time?

"Holly, you feelin' all right, child?" Grandma greeted her. She was frying sausages this morning. The good smell of these made Holly know she was empty.

"Just fine, Grandma. And that smells so good!" She sniffed. As Grandma turned back to watching the sausages, Holly had a chance to meet Judy's gaze. Judy nodded. Which meant that the pillow had worked! Only how soon could they try the maze? Not this morning, with Grandma already lining up what each must do to help in the cleaning out of the stalls.

She and Grandpa had already done a lot, little by little, during the week. But there was still enough left for a busy morning. Grandpa had to go out several times when horns honked and people came to the dump.

The last time he came in he said to Grandma, "Looks like you'd better plan to take off for town a little earlier, Mercy—"

When Holly heard that, her heart sank. Would they have *no* time for the maze at all?

"Mrs. Winton," Grandpa continued, "she sent a message by her boy Alex. They need extra hands to get things ready. Mrs. Pigot and Mrs. Eames, they is down with the flu. Mrs. Winton, she's going in 'bout one-thirty an' she'll pick you up—"

"But that's too early for the young'uns," Grandma said. " 'Course I'll go an' lend a hand. But they won't want to go so early to jus' hang around."

"They can ride in with the Hawkinses. Mrs. Winton, she thought of that. Hawkinses'll come by 'bout a quarter to four an' pick 'em up."

"All right. You be ready, don't keep Mr. Hawkins waitin' none. But then I don't think you will, the party's too special."

Holly could hardly eat her lunch. Grandma said it was amazing how young'uns could get so excited about a party. However, she laughed when she said it. Holly wondered what she would think if she knew that it was not the party at all, but the chance to get to the maze, that made Holly feel as if she were perched on pins and needles and not her proper chair.

Grandma, with the boxes of cookies and doughnuts, left at a quarter to two. As soon as she had driven off, Holly turned to the twins. "We won't have much time later, and getting into those costumes takes time. Suppose we dress up now, and *then* go to the maze."

Crock nodded. "Maybe you've got the right idea. I know it takes a lot of fixing to get into my robot suit."

Grandpa had gone to the fix-it shed, to work on a table he was repairing, so they were free until the Hawkins family would arrive to pick them up. Judy seemed ready to accept Holly's suggestion also, and she did need some help in zippering up her cat costume. That had a pointed-eared head with a cat mask that fitted in neatly over her face. The mask was black and Judy had decided not to try to paint it. She thought she looked like a mixture of Tomkit and a blue-point Siamese. Her tail swung jauntily behind her, and she slipped her hands into the attached paw-mittens, which could be as easily pulled off when she needed the use of her own ten fingers.

Holly put on her robe over her sweater and jeans. She had to roll up the sweater arms and pin them, so they would not show beneath the flowing sleeves of the robe. She had combed her hair out earlier, now all she had to add were the big earrings and the necklaces. But she decided on the final touches of making her lips very red with a lipstick Mom had thrown away and adding some blue dotted lines like tattooing on her forehead and cheeks. The figure that gazed back at her from the mirror was certainly very unlike Holly Wade, whether she was a true African princess or not.

It took both girls to fasten Crock into his square helmet. Then he complained that he could not see, except straight ahead. That was all he needed to, Holly told him firmly, as they set out toward the maze.

This time Tomkit went with them. He was very much interested in Judy's tail, making jumps at it now and then. But, as they came closer to the maze wall, he left off playing to trot ahead with a purposeful air, as if he realized exactly where they were going and why.

Holly knew that the mass of the entwined brush was ahead of them, but she was afraid to look up. What if there were no cats waiting there to watch them, but rather those monsters which had guarded the way she had urged upon them? Also both girls had discovered they had to suit their pace to Crock, his robot costume making any walk over rough ground a clumsy one.

At last, almost defiantly, Holly looked up. She knew a vast relief. Though the cats of brush did not look green as they had the first time the children had come this way, yet they were unmistakably cats and not long-nosed and threatening monsters. This was Tamar's maze, not Hagar's.

Now time was pressing, they must go as quickly as they could. Tomkit had already flashed ahead into the first of the tunnels. Judy, her cat costume looking some-how even more real (as if she were a giant-sized Tomkit), was behind. Then Crock creaked on, and Holly brought up the rear, ready to help if her brother's awkward costume caught on any projections of bush.

As they went the walls did not grow greener, the air

warmer, as had happened the other time. It must be October in the maze instead of summer. Those smaller flowers and bushes, the plants which had given off such a sweet smell when they trod on the old stones of the walk, were withered, with only a stalk here or there to mark where a heavy growth had been.

There were none of the evil-looking toadstools, nor gray ghost plants, which had made the widdershins way so threatening and horrible.

"Can't you hurry, Crock?" Holly almost trod on his heels.

"Listen here, I'm going as fast as I can." His exasperated voice sounded hollowly from inside the robot head. "This suit isn't made for running."

Holly tried to curb her impatience. If they were not back when the Hawkinses came—what then? Judy was already out of sight. But they had only to remember to take each turn on the right. Just the same, it seemed to Holly that they went on for hours before they did come out at last, to see the house and the garden.

That was also withered and frost-touched, but the pool in its center was clear. And the beds had been worked, ready for a new planting. While there were a number of plants which still showed sturdily and had a touch of green. About the beehives there was no sign of life, and they were trussed in straw. The house itself had a snug, ready-for-the-winter look about it.

Though the door was shut, smoke came from the chimney. Judy was already speeding to the door. Who stood beyond: Tamar—or Hagar? Now that she had reached this point, Holly was afraid again to prove herself right—or wrong!

As she steered Crock through the herb garden, Judy

reached up a paw-mittened hand to hammer on that door with a confidence Holly was certainly very far from feeling. However, when the door did open in answer to her knock, it was Tamar who faced them.

She wore a red-brown dress the color of an autumn leaf. Around her shoulders was a cloak of the same color, as if she were about to go out. Sighting them, she stood still in amazement. Suddenly Holly realized that, of course, Tamar had not expected them in costume, if she had looked for them at all. Judy and Crock had masks on, but perhaps Tamar would know her.

"Tamar!" Judy cried that aloud, as Tomkit gave a loud wail. While Holly pushed past Crock—

"Tamar, it's us! Judy, Crock, Holly"—with a stabbing finger she named them all. "Truly it is!"

Then Tamar smiled. "So do I see the truth beneath the disguise. Come thee in! Blessed be, blessed be!"

The house was warm, spicy with smells. Tomkit leaped upon the table to nose into a basin sitting there. Holly was impatient. Tamar must know, understand as soon as possible—

"Tamar—" she began when Judy, fumbling with her cat mask so she could loose it on one side and show her face, interrupted.

"Tamar—Sexton Dimsdale, he is coming with men. They think you're a witch. They want to burn your house, hurt you! Tamar, you've got to get away! It's Halloween and they came on Halloween—" Judy was close to tears.

Tamar looked from Judy to Crock, and, last of all, to Holly. "A witch—" she repeated slowly.

"It's Hagar's fault," Holly burst out then. "She gave Seth Elkins something to put in the medicine you made for his father. She told Seth it would make his father let them get married. But it was bad. It hurt a dog and Sexton Dimsdale saw that. It's all in the old book at the library, I read it. Tamar—you have to—"

Now Tamar's attention was fastened on Holly. "What dost thou know of Hagar?" Her voice was stern, sharp.

Holly flushed. "We came here, we met Hagar. She, she told me I was like her, that I had to help her." Holly swallowed. Under Tamar's steady gaze she felt more and more ashamed of admitting just how much she had wanted the witch wishes and had been eager to do as Hagar asked.

"And how wert thou to help her?" Tamar was still stern of face.

"She gave me some seeds and a root—to plant, back there in our own time."

"And thou did this?"

"Yes. Only—only Judy found they were killing all of Grandma's plants, and the ones you had given her, too. Judy, she spilled all the pots out and mashed the bad things that grew."

They all saw and heard Tamar draw a deep breath. Then she took a step forward and her hand cupped Holly's chin gently, turning up her face. Tamar looked into Holly's eyes, a long, long look without blinking, a look which seemed to Holly to see all the small meannesses, the rebellion, the cheating, which had brought her once to Hagar.

"Aye, thou hast the gift, child. It be more burden than gift, for it do tempt one into dark ways—even as thou ventured. Be grateful to this sister of thine that she did break the spell laid upon thee. It be hard in this world for those who be akin to the power of magic. Sparingly must they ever use it, and only to another's good, never their own.

"Hear then the law, little sister: 'That thou lovest all things in Nature. That thou shalt suffer no person to be harmed by thy hands or in thy mind. That thou walkest humbly in the ways of men and the ways of the gods. Contentment thou shalt at last learn through suffering, and from long patient years, and from nobility of mind and service. For the wise never grow old—' "

"You said part of that once before," Crock said hollowly from within his helmet. "It sounds like—like something out of a church."

"Not from a church as thee knows one, little brother," Tamar replied, "for it is the wisdom of a people worshipping a power older than any church now known. But thee, younger sister,"—she spoke once more directly to Holly—"strive not to reach for that which will lie ahead. In time will it be rightfully revealed to thee. And give thanks to those powers which art of the Right Way, that thou didst not venture so far down the Left that thou couldst not retreat."

"But Tamar"—Judy slipped her hand out of her mitten, caught the edge of Tamar's cloak and gave it a tug —"please, you must be getting away. Those men are coming."

"What say these records of thine own time as to what happened when they did come?"

"That—that some demons appeared while you were talking with Sexton Dimsdale, and the men were frightened and ran. When they came back, the house—everything—was gone!" Holly supplied quickly.

"This be indeed Hallowmas, when the worlds of time

turn counterwise if the power be great enough," Tamar said slowly. She was talking more to herself than to them, Holly thought. "Little one," she said to Judy, "how grow those seeds thou planted?"

"They're all showing," Judy said eagerly. "Some are about that high!" She measured a space with her finger.

"There be a binding tie, then!" Again the children did not understand, but Tamar swept back her cloak to free her arms, leaving it lying in heavy folds on her shoulders. She spun away from them to face the table.

The top of that was less cluttered than it had been the last time they had seen it. There were four red candles at the points of a square, and beyond them two black candles. Within the candle square was a wreath made of colored leaves interwoven with some small flowers: goldenrod; that bright purple one Grandma called "ironweed"; and another, rusty red, which she named "devil's-paintbrush." In the center of the wreath was a metal bowl in which lay some lumps of brown stuff.

Tamar stood for a long moment surveying this, her hands resting on her hips. She might have been Grandpa about to reach for the right tool with which to finish a very difficult piece of carpentry.

"Is my power great enough? How may I know? The proof be in the doing. But when it be the hour for the opening of gates, passage thereby can be two ways, from our world out to our world in. If—"

Holly dared to interrupt. "We've got to get back—to our own time. They'll be looking for us—"

But she was already too late..

"Ho, witch! Show thy ugly face!"

The shout from outside startled them all. Judy was

closest to the window. She looked out over the high sill, which was at her eye level.

"Men—with torches!" she cried out.

Tamar turned away from the table. "But I am warned," she said calmly. "Do ye stay hidden. I know not if aught on this side of time can do ye hurt, but that we shall not put to the proof."

Still calm of manner, she went to the door and opened it, stepping outside, while Holly and Crock crowded beside Judy at the window. Somehow, during the short time they had been within the house, it had grown much darker; it was quite dusk now. Outside, the cruel light of torches made all the frost-killed herb garden plain. Men tramped across its beds, crushing those plants which still showed some life.

Holly shivered. She had never seen such looks on men's faces. That one who stood a little ahead of the rest, he had a sword in his hand. On the bared blade the firelight ran red.

"What seek ye, neighbors?" Tamar stood there, fronting them. The three at the window could not see her face. But Holly, remembering how the panes of the window could be opened, gave a shove to the nearest so they could hear.

"Thou, witch! Death has been ill-brewed in thy pots, death for our good friend Increase Elkins!"

"Where be Master Elkins, so may he say that to my face, as be a matter of the justice due to all?"

"The Holy Writ gives thee proper justice, witch. Does it not say plainly, Suffer not a witch to live?"

There was a kind of growl from the men standing behind Sexton Dimsdale. Judy cowered down with a little cry and Holly flinched. That sound made her more frightened than she had ever been in her life.

"Thou wishes my land, Master Dimsdale, canst thou deny that before a company who many times over have heard thee say this? How better can thee get it than falsely to accuse a healing woman of witchcraft? Think upon that, thou who follow with those bright torches of thine. Aye, I see thee, Reuben Fenester. How would thy goodwife have fared had I not tended her? And here thou standest also, Micah Hawkins, that did come to me with that evil wound which none could heal. Look at the very hand with which thou now holdest that torch. What thou seest there be a clean scar, be that not so?

"And thou, Rupert Briggs, thou hast a son who lives, and not another child laid in the grave. And thou, thou, thou—" Tamar raised her hand to point at man after man. "All are in my debt for lives saved and hurts healed. Yet now thou followest one who, because he covets that which has been proven truly mine, raises the cry of 'witch.' Think well on the past, neighbors—"

"Listen not to her!" Sexton Dimsdale's voice drowned out Tamar's. "Does not the Devil give those he loves council so that they may twist the thoughts of honest men, even as they twist their bodies with vile poisons? Listen to her, and thou art lost to the Devil's ways, as she be deep in them! Have ye not all seen that mastiff which died of the potion she gave unto Elkins? Mad it was, and foaming at the muzzle, so I needs must shoot it lest it savage its own master. What if Elkins had drunk the whole of that? Perhaps death would have seemed sweeter to him than life thereafter? Thou knowest the Holy Writ: Can we pray to a just God when a witch dwells

213 &

in peace among us? What chastening blows may He send upon us for such weak folly?"

There was a sound from the men and they came closer. Holly found she could not look at their faces now. These frightened her so, she was sick. There was a sharp tug at her flowing sleeve—Crock's hand on it!

He had grabbed hold of Judy's tail, to pull her, too.

"Come on!" His voice sounded hollow and strange inside the robot head. Holly saw that his eyes were flashed on, burning brightly. "Come on!"

Holly stumbled toward the door. Judy tried to jerk away, but Crock shoved her ahead of him.

"Open the door!" hissed Crock. "We're going out!"

Out there—? Crock must be crazy. Tamar had told them to stay under cover. Those men—they would catch them—

"Get going!" Crock sounded so fierce this time, Holly did stumble forward to put her hands on the door. "Now listen," his voice boomed on, "when Holly gets that door open, we go out. We yell like crazy—just yell! Understand!"

It was only then that Holly did. Costumed as they were, coming out yelling—the demons! Were *they* the demons who had frightened off the attack on Tamar? But that had happened long ago—Holly's head was full of mixed-up thoughts which she had no time to straighten out.

Instead, she gave a quick pull to the door, bringing it widely open. Following Crock's orders she leaped forward, voicing the best scream she could summon. There was an echoing bellow, which issued from Crock as he moved more stiffly and slowly toward Tamar. Judy gave a wild yowl not unlike that which Tomkit could utter, but in greater volume.

For a long moment the men stared at the three weird apparitions. Holly was jumping up and down, throwing her arms wide in the air, screeching in rough imitation of an African witch doctor she had seen on TV in a travel program. Crock marched with the stiffness of the robot he hoped to resemble, still bellowing. Judy, as if all her fear had left her, leapt back and forth, her clawed paw-mittens outstretched as if to reach Sexton Dimsdale.

But Master Dimsdale was retreating. Behind him there was a flurry as men broke, turned, and ran, throwing their torches from them. Sexton Dimsdale shouted after them. But, before Crock's steady advance, he retreated until he, too, ran.

"Get those torches!" Crock yelled. "Throw dirt on them. They'll start a fire!"

For the next few moments Holly and Judy were busy—Crock, clumsy in his stiff suit, being able to give little help. When they were sure that the last smoldering spark was out, they went back to the house.

Tamar was inside, but with her—Holly shrank back. She wanted to turn and run, but she felt that if she did, she would indeed be lost.

Hagar stood on the other side of the table, smiling and nodding. "Thus it shall be, Sister!"

"Shall it?" Tamar asked. "Thou hast foreseen this then, and what else?"

"That Sexton Dimsdale shall pray to his God until his knees are raw from the kneeling, but my curse shall not pass from him. And that I, dear sister, shall walk the halls of time to a better day, one more fitting to my purposes. Then I, and not thou, shalt be Lady of the Power. And I shall use it, Sister; ah, how I shall use it!"

"Thou hast seen much—"

"Seen much, and done much, Sister. She who takes the power with a steady hand and a strong purpose (and thou art not such a one) can be Queen and ruler! Mine the kingdom to come!" Hagar's green eyes glowed as if small fires were set in them. "Aye, I have brought thee to this—for it be power linked which will take me where I would be: thy power linked with mine. Thou wilt use the spell of time-warp because thou must or die. Then thou wilt live in thy own forgotten pocket of time. Aye, there thou shalt have thy peace. Since we are blood kin, that I must allow. But I shall be free, and Dimsdale shall continue cursed. For until the maze of time which be now our cage be utterly destroyed, I shall have only half life."

"Thou art very sure of *thy* power to bespeak me so," Tamar said slowly.

"Has not the Left Path always proved to have more force than the Right in the ways of mankind? There be a vast ocean of darkness in their world, for those born of Adam incline to fear and dark by their very nature. Upon their fears can we draw. Hecate of Hell be always the victor in set battle—"

"Believe thee as thou wilt, still thou hast broken the Law. And I fear me thou wilt find that no small thing to be easily forgot."

"The Law? There be more than one law, Sister. And this be Hallowmas when the dead be free to walk again with kin and friend, when the Left waxes the greater. Yet it be also the time we both must use our skill or perish utterly from the malice of those who understand nothing."

Slowly, reluctantly, Tamar inclined her head. "So mote it be."

Hagar laughed. "How thou dost hate to say that, Sister. But thou hast been so simple of wit. *I* have foreseen this hour, *I* have built well toward it—" She darted a glance at Holly, and the girl realized that Hagar knew she had been there all the time.

"The old blood dies not, even in the future," Hagar continued. "There be those whose spirit quickens to answer when the power summons, who are ready to obey."

Tamar did not look at the children at all. "We shall do what must be done. Though what shall come of it—"

Hagar interrupted her. "What will come of it? Peace for you, Sister, with life eternal within thy pocket of time. Mayhap thou will find it dull therein when there be none but thee. Then thou shalt wish that thou wert free, as I shall surely be."

"I wish nothing," Tamar answered, "but that which be my portion. Nor can thee obtain more than that, either."

"Ah, but I have foreseen and foredone. And my portion will be well to my liking. But the time glass speeds its sand; shall we to the business now, Sister?"

Tamar only nodded. Hagar stooped to the hearth fire and, with tongs, picked up a coal which she dropped into the bowl standing wreathed upon the table. Then, swiftly plucking forth another and smaller coal, she lit the candles.

From the bowl rose up a straight thread of smoke which curled as it thickened. Holly could smell a heavy fragrance, as if what Hagar now had set afire gave out perfume. She wanted out of this house, back to the world she knew. Yet she could not move, she could only stand and watch. The smoke grew more and more, and denser, until she could see neither Tamar nor Hagar fronting each other across the table where sat the bowl.

However, she could hear chanting out of that cloud, though she could no longer understand the words. Or could she? For once in a while she had a flash of truer hearing, though never afterward could she remember what had been said. Sometimes her body throbbed queerly, and she felt a forward pull, as if she must push into that cloud of smoke. However, her fear held her where she was.

The chant soared high into the air. Now it seemed that others besides Tamar and Hagar must be there. Other voices, strange ones, joined in. Holly looked to Crock, to Judy. But they were beside her and not in the cloud. Who—who else was there? And how had those others come?

Through the cloud Holly could see the candles, their flames faint spots of light. Then—suddenly—the outermost, those two which were black, went out. There was a cry from the cloud, a wailing scream. Loud at first, it grew fainter and fainter, until there was nothing, only silence.

The cloud began to draw in upon itself, just as it had once flowed out, growing denser at its core, yet allowing more and more of the room to become visible. It became a ball which fell back into the basin and vanished.

Tamar stood there. Her eyes were closed; her hands were stretched out, palms down, over the basin. But—Hagar was gone!

Tamar began to speak, and what she said was like a prayer:

> "Dread Lord, thou who giveth life with one hand and the peace of death with the other, open wide thy gate through which all must, on their appointed day, pass. Giver of peace and rest, do thee take her to thee now, who comes against her will. Let her in the appointed time be born again, that what be done be undone, the wrong made right. And may she then be as fair of spirit as she was of face and form.
>
> *"By all the powers of land and sea,*
> *As I do say, 'So mote it be.'*
> *By all the might of Moon and Sun,*
> *As I do will, let it be done."*

She opened her eyes at last, and leaning closer to the table, she snuffed out the candles from west to east. When she turned to face the children, her face was very pale. And she had to put out her hand to hold the back of the chair, for she swayed as she stood.

"So mote it be," Tamar repeated. "Blessed be, Hagar, for thou wert once a bonny, happy maid. May it be thus for thee again."

"Is—is Hagar dead?" Holly asked, unable for the moment to believe that what she saw and heard was true.

Tamar gave a start, as if she had forgotten all about them. Now she looked directly at Holly very gravely. "What ignorant men call death, little sister, be only a gate to elsewhere, elsewhen. Hagar believed that with her ties to thy time, through those potent things she gave thee to plant, she might reach thy world. Perhaps they might have helped her so—I do not know, for I do not walk her way of knowledge. Since the plants did not flourish, she released her hold here, but had naught to draw her through to there. Thus she has returned to that from which her life spark first came. And I—I also am free—"

"You—where are *we*?" Holly demanded then, fear growing in her. If Tamar had taken off, the house, everything, as the old story had told it—then they must have gone along! They could never get back! She wanted to scream out her terror as that thought struck her.

"Thou be strong-tied to thine own time, little sister. Do not hold such a fear. When thou goest through that door, then thou art free also. Except for such bonds as thou thyself may choose to draw around thee. But I be free of time, even as Hagar, only in a different fashion. And all Dimsdale shall be free of the curse which she did lay upon it."

Judy crept closer. "You—we won't see you again, Tamar?"

Tamar smiled. The weariness, and the shadow of pain, were gone from her face. Plain? Now Tamar was beautiful as Hagar, but in a different way. She threw wide her arms and laughed, not as Hagar had done, spitefully and in anger, but joyfully.

"Time be not easily played with, child. No, we do not meet again. But"—Tamar leaned forward now and touched Judy's forehead with her fingertip—"to thee do I leave such of my arts as thou dost wish to gather to thee. A healer shalt thou be in thine own time, even if thou wilt work that skill in another fashion than my own. Guard thee well, and tend to thy best, those plants which thou hadst from me. As they do grow and wax stronger, shall that which man has reft from this earth without taking heed of his selfishness, begin to return.

For these all be blessed things such as restore, not harm. In growth there be life, if that growth be truly rooted in this earth, and not from the fevered imaginings of men who believe themselves beyond the ancient laws.

"To thee, brave heart"—she turned now to Crock—"do I say that courage be a gift mightier than any I can give. But"—she reached behind her to the table and picked up a small spatter of wax which had dripped from one of the candles—"thy hands shall know skill and shall make things which will not only serve thy fellows well, but shall hold beauty. Take this, and it shall be an amulet to bring thee much, but only through thine own endeavors."

"For you, Sister"—she spoke at last to Holly—"ah, I give thee welcome to the heart hold. And *this*, which thou shalt find, if thou dost wish it rightfully, will be what thou seeketh."

She had taken something else from the table: a small book, its cover seeming made of thin sheets of wood, with a metal clasp to hold it tight-shut. Holly took it from her almost reluctantly. She had a very odd feeling that if she opened it—when she opened it (for she knew that she would)—life would never quite be the same again.

"Merry meet, merry part." Tamar drew down her cloak about her shoulders. "The time be short. Blessed be throughout thy days—"

The door opened behind them, though none of the three had touched it. Though they tried to say good-bye, they could not find the words. They went out into the open—then—

Garden, house—they were gone. The hedges, all of the maze, had closed in about them. Yet there was a clear opening in it where Tomkit waited. When he saw them, he mewed loudly and started on. It was like being in a dream, Holly thought. She did not want to talk about it, and apparently neither did Judy or Crock.

Suddenly Crock said, "I wonder what time it is."

"The Hawkinses—maybe they've come!" Judy, her tail bobbing, started to run.

Holly had forgotten the party. Now she remembered with a rush of excitement. They must not be too late! She set her hand on Crock's arm, hurrying him along. Just as they made the final turn and came out of the maze, they could hear the beeping of a horn.

The Hawkinses! Holly hitched up her robe, stuffed the book under the belt of her jeans for safekeeping, and rounded the house with Crock who was shuffling forward at the pace his costume would allow.

11   Lavender's Green— Blessed Be!

It was as if they had awakened from a dream. To join in the party in town made them almost forget what had happened. And when Crock won first prize for the most unusual costume, they were all excited. When Grandpa

came for them with the truck, they were so tired they
flopped down together in the back. But, as they went,
suddenly Judy began to sing:

> "Lavender's blue, dilly, dilly!
> Lavender's green.
> When I am king, dilly, dilly!
> Thou shalt be queen."

"Tamar's a queen," she said softly. "In her own place
now, she is a queen. And I'm going to do what she said.
I'm going to be a healing woman, a real doctor!"

"You got to spend a long time learning that," Crock
commented. "She said the curse has gone from Dimsdale.
I wonder, will that help Grandpa keep the dump?"

Holly's hands were at her middle. She could feel the
book, which pressed against her right there. Crock's
question made her realize that they had come from the
troubles in the strange maze world only to face the
troubles of their own. She was very tired, and, now that
the excitement of the party was past, she was worried
again.

"We've got to do something." Her old impatience to be
in action had awakened.

"What?" Crock asked with good reason. Judy, lost in
her own dream of the future, hummed again the tune of
the song.

"Well—" Holly had not really thought past the fact
that they must do. Only, Crock was very right: What
could they do?

"We've got to think of something," she said, knowing
that that was a very feeble sort of an answer.

"All right, we think." Crock had had them help him
off with his robot head, which he now balanced on his

knee. "Grandpa, Grandma, they've been acting as if nothing's going to happen. If we have to move, where will we go?"

His question roused Judy from her own dream. "Go? We can't go anywhere, Crock. We have to plant Tamar's things, and have a garden like hers. We promised!"

"So? Then you do some thinking, too," Crock returned.

There was no more humming, nor even talking. Think —what could anyone do if Sussex did not care? If the town voted out the dump, and turned the land over to Mr. Reuther? All Grandpa's young trees, Grandma's herbs, the maze—Holly stiffened. The maze! Surely that was unusual. Suppose they could open it up again, make it the way it had been long ago, with an herb garden in the center? Grandma knew all the garden-club ladies. She went to their meetings herself, and they came to her when they had questions about herbs. Holly had heard all that from Judy when she was putting down ideas in her project book.

Would the garden-club ladies be interested enough to want to save the Dimsdale maze? What about the Cub Scouts and the older troop? They came out for their toy project. There was Mr. Correy, and Mr. Lem—how many other people would be on their side?

However, she did not demand attention now from the twins as she would have done once. Make a plan, a real plan, and then show them. So far she had only the beginnings of such a plan.

When they got home they went upstairs to take off their costumes. Tomkit lay on Judy's bed, his head resting on the maze pillow. He was purring gently in his sleep.

"He's dreaming, too," Judy laughed, "and good dreams.

But he's got to move over and give me some room to sit."
She lifted the cat so gently, he did not wake as she put
him closer to the other side of the bed. When she picked
up the pillow, somehow it fell out of her hand, and
rolled over to lie at Holly's feet.

Holly stooped to take it up. The maze lines were on it.
But, as she absently turned it over, she saw that the other
maze pattern, which had led her to Hagar, was gone!
Instead there was a spray of flowers embroidered in time-
dulled colors as if they had always been there.

"Judy"—Holly was too astounded to believe what she
saw—"do you see this?" She dangled the pillow before
her sister.

Judy inspected the embroidery with intent interest.
"That's lavender"—she pointed to the tallest of the flower
stalks. "This is bee balm, and that's an old, old kind of
rose they used to use a lot, they called it 'damask.' This
is dill—this greenish bit, and that's bittersweet with the
orange berries. The rest, I don't know. But I'll look them
up in the herb book. They're all good things, Holly, the
kind Tamar would have in her garden."

"But the pattern of Hagar's maze, it's gone!" Holly
could not see why Judy took this so calmly. Embroidery
did not just change in a few hours, it could not! And these
flowers were so faded, they looked as if they had been
sewn there at the same time as the other maze pattern.

"It had to go, didn't it?" Judy asked calmly. "It was part
of Hagar's magic. And when she went, there was no more
use for it." Judy ran her finger up and down the center-
most stalk of the flower she identified as lavender. "Lavender *is* blue, or sort of lavender-blue, and it's green before
the flowers come out. Grandma has some. She told me
that Miss Elvery showed her once how to make lavender

fans for summer. You get real thin lavender material and sew stalks of dried lavender between two layers for ribs! I'm going to try that this summer. I'm going to make rose beads, like Tamar's, and tussie-mussies," she said dreamily. "There's so much to know, Holly, so much to know in this world! I wish I knew all that Tamar does."

Holly had washed her face; now she was trying to comb her wild brush of hair into order. She wanted to be Holly Wade right here in Dimsdale, in Sussex, not an African princess.

"Nobody could know everything," she said a little shortly. "Not even Tamar."

"No," Judy agreed. "But she knew things maybe we don't know today. Holly, she gave you that book, maybe that has things in it—"

Holly glanced at the drawer in the chest where she had put the book a few minutes ago, pushed well down to the bottom beneath her underclothing. She had a queer feeling about that book. Sometimes she was excited to think of opening it, but mostly she was afraid. Afraid that if she did, she would be another person, not the Holly Wade she had always known.

"You might look," Judy continued. She padded across the floor in her furry slippers to return the pillow once more to her box of cloth pieces. "There's no harm in just looking—"

Now she had to. With Judy watching, Holly could not allow herself to admit that she was afraid, afraid to open the old book. To keep Judy from suspecting this, Holly marched resolutely to the drawer, unearthed the book. She sat down at the foot of her bed and really closely examined it for the first time.

The covers were thin pieces of wood, but the spine was

leather. The volume was fastened securely shut with a metal clasp such as Holly had never seen on a book before, quite unlike the strap and lock which her diary had. She pulled at the metal very gingerly, not even sure that the hasp was not locked in some way. However, at her touch the metal pieces slid easily apart.

Holly, that mingled tingle of excitement and fear growing all the stronger in her, lifted the cover. The pages did not feel like paper, either. They were thicker than any paper she had ever seen, and a deep yellow.

Inside was writing, not printing—writing she could not read! As she turned the pages, she found drawings, too, in the form of stars and odd-shaped crosses. The old writing went around them as if explaining. But Holly could not make out a single word she knew. Her disappointment was deep. She flicked over the next page with a growing impatience. It was loose and slipped from the book onto the bed. Then she saw the sheet had not been a page at all, but a separate paper, very brown, which had been folded and tucked in tightly there.

A little bit of the edge flaked off as she tried to pick it up, and she was afraid of tearing it to bits before she could even see what it was. Then she had an idea. Her new photograph album had clear sheets between which one could set pictures—she might put this whole page in there, but she would have to be very careful.

"What's that?" Judy leaned over to look at the find.

"Don't touch it!" ordered Holly. "It's so old, it's coming apart. I'm going to try this." She put down the unreadable book and found the photograph album, opening it to an unused page. "If I can get it unfolded," she explained, "without it tearing all up, we can put it in here."

"I'll hold the book for you!" Judy offered.

Holly had never worked with such care. This was how Grandma probably had to do it when she mended the broken china. Luckily most of what flaked off was just around the edge, and she was able to get the sheet spread out without losing much. There was a drawing on it, too, but she did not stop to examine it closely. Instead she worked as fast as she could to get it under the plastic covering in the album.

When that was done at last, she held it closer to the lamp. This was a drawing of the maze! Done in far more detail than the embroidery on the pillow. In the center of rings of paths was a small garden, just like the one which had been in front of Tamar's house. But there was no house. And around the outer walls of the maze were lines of flower beds. Some were very strange-looking, for the flowers had been planted to form square knots or other geometric shapes.

There was a lot of lettering. Perhaps, Holly guessed, the names of the flowers and shrubs which were supposed to be planted in each bed. However, at the bottom were much larger words, ones she could read: "Ye Garden as be made for Dimsdale, in ye year 1683, by Master Herbert Truelow."

A picture of the garden, the Dimsdale garden which Tamar's father had made! Holly ran her finger over the plastic sheet protecting the very old drawing. "Judy, I'm going to copy this, for my project report. But this ought to be in the museum where everyone can see it. I'll bet there isn't another garden like this, with a maze and all, in the whole state of Massachusetts—maybe not even in the whole country! I wonder how much of it we can still see?"

"There's the maze, if we could get in." Judy bumped

heads with Holly, she was so eager to get closer to look at the page. "Grandpa, Grandma, they might know—"

Carefully Holly loosened the plastic page from the album. And, when they heard Grandma's dinner bell, she carried it with her downstairs. She was already thinking about what she would say when they asked her where she found it. To tell about Tamar's book—no, she could not do that. But she could say, and it would be true, that she found it folded in the pages of an old book. Grandma knew she had been going through the books on Grandma's library shelves, and some were very old.

"Shouldn't think you young'uns 'd want much to eat tonight," Grandpa said when he had finished saying grace, "seein' as how you had all those party fixin's."

"An' eat all of 'em did," Grandma announced. "Not only ourn but all the rest. Seems like young'uns get empty clean down to their toe-tips.

"I was right proud of you," she continued. "Miss Sarah an' Mrs. Beach, an' Mrs. Hawkins, they all came up to me to say as how them costumes of yours were awfully good. Mrs. Dale, she wants the pattern for the cat one, Judy. Says as how they're fixin' to give a play at Christmas time with Puss-in-Boots, an' she never did see such a lifelike-lookin' cat as you turned out to be. Yes, the party was grand, all of it."

But to Holly the party was already far in the past. It was the present, and the plan she was working on, which were of the first importance. She waited for Grandpa to finish his soup and start in on his brown bread and jelly. Then she could wait no longer. "Grandpa, does any of the old garden here still show? I know the maze is there all grown up and tight, but the rest of it?"

He took what seemed to Holly an extra long moment to

answer. "Well now, it's hard to tell. There's some old lilacs, like trees now. But they weren't planted that long ago. Oaks maybe—I jus' dunno."

Holly felt a swift disappointment. If *none* of the old garden was there, then no one would be interested in keeping it. The maze—there was only the maze left!

"Grandpa, could you sort of tame the maze, find the old way in and out?" She held on to that last hope.

"The maze!" Grandma was staring at her.

But Grandpa looked interested. "Funny you say that right now, Holly. I was goin' 'round the edge o' that this afternoon. An' there was a dead bit which sorta hung out. I don't know why I gave it a tug, but I did. An' a whole big lot of it came loose, jus' like I pulled me out a cork. Inside there was a path, a paved path. It warn't near as growed together in there as we always thought, neither."

"Miss Elvery," cut in Grandma, "she said as how we should keep away from that."

"Miss Elvery has been gone to her rest a good long time now, Mercy. Anyways—it always looked so dark an' dismal-like, I didn't have much use for it. But this evenin', well, it was different somehow. I got the feelin', with just a little prunin' an' the like, it could be opened up agin."

Holly reached under the table edge for the sheet of plastic lying on her knees. "Grandpa, I found a kind of map—of how the garden used to be. It was in an old book, all folded up, and just fell out. Look here!"

He took the page and held it closer to the lamp. "I do declare. Mercy, you remember that there book as you found for Miss Sarah, the big one from the Winslow place what they tore down to build the motel 'cross the river? That had all them queer oldish pictures 'bout gardens an' such. Well, this here might be right outta that."

Grandma took the page in turn, rammed up her glasses high and hard on her nose. "It sure do look a little like 'em, Luther."

"I'm going to copy it for my project," Holly said. "But Grandpa, mazes—they aren't common in gardens, at least 'round here, are they?"

"Never did hear tell of one 'cept this."

"Then it would be important to have one to show people," Holly persisted. "People like the garden clubbers and the Scouts, and the people coming to the Sussex birthday celebration. It says on here that this was made in 1683. That's almost as old as the town, awfully old—"

Grandpa had stopped eating. He reached out and took the page back from Grandma, holding the sheet quite close to his nose as if to get a better look at every small detail.

"Th' town meetin'"—it was Grandma who spoke first. "Luther, if the maze could be opened an', like Holly says, showed off right—"

Slowly Grandpa nodded. "It's a good thought, Mercy. Monday mornin' I gets me out there to see what good such thinkin' can do us."

"You turn right to get to the center," Judy said.

Holly was scared at her sister's thoughtlessness. Now they would ask how she could possibly know that. She thought the question was actually forming on Grandma's lips.

"You know how I know?" Judy continued, making, as far as Holly could see, bad matters much worse. " 'Cause it's on the pillow—wait—"

She pushed free of the table, rushed for the stairs, disappearing above.

"Oh th' pillow, what does that young'un mean?" Grandpa

asked. He looked to Holly for an answer and she could not find one. But Judy was coming back so fast, she almost tripped on the stairs. In one hand she held the pillow, which she gave to Grandma, who was the nearest, and with her finger she traced the lines of embroidery. "Look at the picture, then at this! See—they are the same. If you just keep turning right each time, you find the center!"

"I do believe she's right!" Grandma traced the way with her own finger, then got up to lean over Grandpa's shoulder to do the same on the plastic above the drawing. "An' mazes—they is uncommon, Luther. When Mrs. Holmes went with the garden clubbers from Boston on that there tour two springs ago, she told us all about one she saw in Virginia. They thought that was so important, people came from 'way off just to walk through it. They had to pay money to visit it an' the man who owned the place, he used the money to keep it in shape, hiring gardeners an' all. Luther, if there be anything th' Selectmen would relish, it would be a way of makin' money, 'specially durin' this birthday week they is so set on havin'. Everybody in town is tryin' to think of ways to help out. Mr. Correy, he's goin' to open th' old blacksmithin' part of his shop an' have a blacksmith there to make things—an'— But you've heard 'em all a-talkin' 'bout this. Now you do some nosin' into the maze, an' if you think as how we can make somethin' unusual, we'll tell Mrs. Correy an' Mr. Bill. That'll give 'em somethin' excitin' to say at the town meetin'! Luther, you take that there picture in to Miss Sarah on Monday. She'll be excited too. Me, I'm goin' to tell Mrs. Pigot an' Mrs. Holmes. She will be sure surprised what we got right here an' you don't got to go to Virginia to see, neither!"

Holly felt a shade of disappointment. After all, she had found the garden map, and no one seemed to remember that. Then she thought about the other parts of the plan. She would tell Mrs. Finch and Mrs. Dale. Crock, he could talk to the Scouts. They'd just have to organize, see that plenty of people would go to the town meeting—

She thought it would be hard to get to sleep that night, she had so many things to think about. But it was not. Instead she slipped right into a strange dream, one which she was able to remember in detail when she woke, as one seldom remembers a dream.

She had been in Tamar's house and it welcomed her; she felt as if she had come home to her own place. Tamar was there, sitting in the tall-backed chair at the table. She did not glance at Holly, or speak to her. Yet the girl was sure that Tamar did know she was there. But what she was doing was so important that she must not be disturbed.

Tamar's elbows rested on the table, her hands supporting her chin, as she gazed into a mirror which had been laid flat before her. Only Tamar was not reflected in that mirror, nor was anything else about her. Instead the surface was covered with a silvery cloud which billowed and changed.

Holly felt the force of Tamar's will, for she was willing something to happen.

When Holly looked down onto the clouded mirror, it made her feel queer and dizzy, and she could not do it for long. But Tamar sat there so still, you hardly knew she breathed, willing—

The cloudiness became a shape. For a single moment Holly thought she saw a face clear and bright. Then the cloud returned. Tamar sighed, leaning weakly back against the tall support of the chair. Her eyes were closed. Holly longed to go to her. Only, in this dream world she was rooted to the floor. That mirrored face—had she really seen, in Tamar's strange mirror, a small, clear reflection of her *father*?

How could her father have come to Tamar's house? Though Holly looked almost wildly around the room now in search, he was not there. But at that moment Tamar's eyes opened. She looked straight at Holly, catching her own gaze, holding it fast. Holly saw Tamar's lips shape words. Though she could not hear them, she knew exactly what those words were:

> *"By all the powers of land and sea,*
> *As I do say, 'So mote it be.'*
> *By all the might of moon and sun,*
> *As I will, it shall be done!"*

Then, again, more slowly, with a pause between each word as if to impress the message on Holly's memory: "So mote it be!"

Tamar's hand was raised; her fingers moved in the air tracing a sign which glowed for an instant, as if she had written so with fire. And then—

Holly awoke in her own bed. The dark was complete. Around her were the sounds of the barn-house—as if it reassured itself each night, when no one was awake to hear, that it was still standing sturdy and complete.

Holly's lips shaped Tamar's last message. "So mote it be!" She had not a single doubt that she knew its meaning. There would be another telegram. Oh, maybe not tomorrow, or next week, or even next month, but there would *be* one—a good one, this time. Then their own small world would change again, from the dark Left to the sunny Right. Wherever Tamar now was, she had worked her own magic for Dad. He would be coming home!

However, now it was left to Holly to work magic, too—the magic for Dimsdale. She did not have Tamar's powers, she had only her own will and whatever she could think of. But as she willed, it should be done!

They did not have a chance on Sunday morning to go out and see the maze. Sunday was church day, again Holly must curb her impatience. She knew also that she could not share, even with Judy, her last dream. Somehow she was very certain that it would break Tamar's magic if she talked about it.

After they had eaten dinner Grandpa seemed restless. He did not sit down to leaf through his pile of old garden catalogs, which he always did when he was settled for a quiet time.

Grandma asked finally, "What's got into you, Luther? You're like a cat on hot bricks. There's somethin' a-botherin' you."

"I know it's Sunday, Mercy. But I've got me the need to go lookin' at that there maze. Not to do any work on it, just give it a look. I don't know why it sticks in my mind this here way, only it do."

Grandma did not answer him at once. She got up from the chair where she had settled herself with a number of *National Geographic*s to hand.

"Funny you should say that, Luther. Th' very same thing's been runnin' in my mind. All right, suppose we all go an' take us a look. Tomorrow I'm to fetch some cookin' herbs over to Mrs. Holmes. Could be if I had somethin' real to tell her, she'd come out for a look 'fore the town meetin'."

So they all followed Grandpa to where he had found the break in the maze wall. Holly looked for the two cats on guard. And she was sure, though the brush had grown up a lot, that she could still trace there the old outlines of both. She did not know how they could be drawn to Grandpa's attention later, or whether he could make anything of them again, but they *were* there, only waiting to be freed from what had grown about them.

Between those hidden guardians was the entrance, where they could indeed see a paved walk through a tunnel of green, far more open than one would think upon viewing the matted and tangled outer wall. There was nothing alarming or forbidding about that opening, and Grandpa stepped right in.

"Might as well see," he said over his shoulder, "just how far in we can get. But it's clearer than outside—"

He took the first right turn. Again the way was reasonably open. It was as if the maze had been waiting just for them to come exploring. Now and then Grandma stopped to stoop and finger a stalk of frost-killed plant or pick up a dried leaf.

"There was a regular wall of lavender here, Luther," she cried excitedly. "An' here's mint, I do believe; an' that there's surely thyme! The bushes must give all this shelter. Rosemary—that there's true rosemary!"

Again they made a turn. At the fourth turn some failure of the growth made the tall cats stand out clearly. Grandpa stopped short to stare at them.

"Now whatever's here?" he demanded. "Lookit this, all of you: the bushes cut to make them! I never seen th' like." Suddenly he paused. "That ain't quite so—'member that *Geographic* picture, Mercy? Th' one about that garden what's in England where all them bushes were cut up careful to be birds, an' animals? Tomorrow"—he was clearly growing more excited—"I'm goin' right in an' get Mr. Correy. He ain't no gardener, but he knows 'bout old things. He'll sure be surprised to see this here."

"Maybe there're others," Crock suggested. "They might be grown over some. If they were to be cut again—"

"Surely!" Grandpa nodded excitedly. "Only it will take some figurin' how to do that just right, without spoilin' 'em none. It would have to be done real careful."

Grandma held her glasses tightly in place as she viewed the brush cats.

"Now that there," she announced, "wasn't in that Virginia maze. This beats that other maze all to pieces. Luther, you can get Mr. Correy, but you'll have to bring out Mrs. Holmes, too. She will sure be taken back to find you don't have to go clear to Virginia to see this!"

Grandpa seemed reluctant to leave the cats, but Holly urged him on. She was sure that there was no longer any house caught within the maze, but she was eager to see what did lie there now.

Three more turns and they came out into the open. Though there was a thick growth here now, of sere and withered plants, lines could still be traced to show Tamar's ordered garden. And there was the pool, a small slick of ice still at its bottom.

Grandma fell upon the remains of the plants, excitedly identifying them from brittle leaves, or stalk.

"This was just a big herb garden, Luther. 'Course a lotta what was once here must be dead. But lookit all what kept growin' all these years. It's hard to believe it could, Luther, 'cept we know there weren't no way any-one could get in to plant an' tend it. Why, we can plant it again. An' it will be somethin' as no one hereabouts has ever seen in their born days!"

A hand slipped into Holly's. She turned her head, Judy was smiling broadly. Crock, his hand holding Judy's other one, was grinning. Without quite knowing that she said it, Holly whispered, "So mote it be!"

She was as sure at that moment that Dimsdale was safe as she was that someday their father would come. She remembered Tamar's farewell to them:

"Blessed be!" And she did say that more loudly, but neither Grandpa or Grandma seemed to hear her. Only Judy and Crock nodded with vigor and certainty that that would come true—Dimsdale was no longer cursed, but blessed.

To Make Tamar's Rose Beads and Other Old Delights

ફ⊌ ROSE BEADS

Choose fully open roses with a strong scent; dark red are best. Remove petals only and put these in a strong crockery bowl. Using a heavy utensil (the handle of an all-metal ice-cream scoop is excellent), crush the petals into a thick paste.

Roll the paste into beads, which can then be strung on thread with a sharp needle. Or put them in a small nylon net bag for use in drawers as sachet. But dry them well first. The fragrance will last a long time.

৯ TASTIES FOR TEA

Take a good-sized, thick-skinned orange and mark the skin with a knife into quarters. Peel these away from the fruit. With the knife, scrape the white inner side of the peel as clean as you can. Then cut into small squares about three-quarters of an inch in size.

Into each square push a stick of clove. And then allow to dry. Keep in a closed tin box or jar. Drop into hot tea for special flavor.

৯ SUGARED MINT LEAVES

Pick mint before the flowers bloom. Select the medium-sized leaves, not the large ones near the bottom of the stem, nor the too-small upper ones. Wash and dry by laying out on a paper towel.

Take the white of one egg and beat it slightly, until it is frothy. Dip the leaves into the egg and then into a saucer of sugar.

Spread on a sheet of foil and put in oven at the lowest degree of heat until each leaf is dry. Keep in tightly closed bottle or jar. These may be eaten as candy, or used to flavor either hot or cold tea.

৯ POMANDER BALL

Select a well-shaped, medium-sized orange. Using Scotch tape, mark it off into halves lengthwise. Get two small boxes of whole cloves.

Using an ice pick, make holes between the tape lines very close together and insert a clove into each until no skin can be seen at all.

Pull off the tape and put ribbon in its place, so that the ball may be hung in a closet if you wish. This will last for a long time and give a fine spicy scent. Pomander balls were often used in linen cupboards.

LITTLE FUZZY

&

THE CLASSIC SEQUEL TO THE SCIENCE FICTION BESTSELLER *LITTLE FUZZY!*

FUZZY SAPIENS

Too long out of print, these delightful SF classics are finally available to the legions of readers waiting to discover the new human race — Fuzzy Sapiens!

Available wherever paperbacks are sold or use this coupon.